RACING AND ROBBERIES

DUNE HOUSE COZY MYSTERY

CINDY BELL

CHAPTER 1

Mary tossed the car keys from one hand to the other as she attempted to remember exactly what she needed from the store. Just a moment before she knew what it was, and now, she hadn't the faintest idea. As she looked around the kitchen she hoped that something might jog her memory. What she could remember, was that it was important, and needed before the guests arrived in the afternoon.

"Mary?" Suzie's voice drifted into the kitchen from the living room. "Have you seen the car keys?"

"I have them." Mary stepped out of the kitchen and met Suzie in the living room. "I need to go to the store for something, but I can't remember what.

I'm telling you, Suzie, I think I'm really starting to lose it."

"Oh stop, you'll never lose it, Mary. But I do need the car keys." She held her hand out. "I need to pick something up in town, before Paul gets in tonight."

"Well, maybe we can go together? I know I needed something." Mary's voice trailed off as she searched her memory for what it might have been.

"Honestly, I had planned to do quite a few errands." Suzie pursed her lips. "You know, I think maybe we need to revisit the idea of getting a second car. It really doesn't work for us to have to share all of the time."

"You're right." Mary dropped the keys into Suzie's outstretched palm. "It seemed like a money-saver at the time, but now that we're so busy with guests and other activities it gets to be a bit of a scheduling strain. I actually know of someone who is selling a nice SUV. I think it might work well to drive our guests around on the odd occasion as well, because it will have plenty of room. Plus, there would be room to haul things when we want to redecorate the rooms, or do some extra landscaping."

"That's a great idea." Suzie's eyes lit up with the

thought. "I've always wanted to have something to haul my antique finds in. Sometimes I turn down an item just because I don't want to have to pay the added fee for delivery."

"Then it's decided. Why don't I ride into town with you to look at it? I can always find another way home."

"I'll give you a lift back if we don't buy it. Don't worry, I can postpone a few things. Let's go take a look at this SUV." Suzie looped her arm through Mary's. "Now, we have to decide who gets the car and who gets the SUV."

"Uh, I think that depends on who gets the keys first." Mary grinned as she eyed her friend.

"Hmm, good plan."

"Have you seen Pilot?" Mary had last seen their yellow Labrador when they returned from their morning walk.

"He's in the yard." Suzie peered through the kitchen window to make sure he was there. "He's having a nap." She laughed.

"Great."

"Let's go." Suzie pushed open the door of Dune House and led Mary out onto the porch. The sight of the beautiful beach outstretched beyond the hill that the large bed and breakfast sat on, took Suzie's breath away as always. It had been some time since she'd inherited the property from an uncle she barely knew, and decided to enlist her best friend to help her turn it into its former glory as a bed and breakfast, but she still felt a subtle shock of joy when she realized that view belonged to her. "What time are the guests arriving today?"

"Around two. They all said that they weren't going to be around for dinner, so I am going to make a lunch spread for them, instead. Oh, that's it!" Mary snapped her fingers. "I need to get some tomatoes for the sandwiches, the ones we had in the fridge have gone bad."

"See, I knew you would figure it out." Suzie winked at her as she opened the car door.

"I'm glad I did." Mary sighed as she eased her way into the passenger side. In her fifties, she felt very old next to her best friend, who was nearly the same age. Suzie looked so young with her tanned skin, and brassy blond hair. Yes, she dyed it, but that wasn't the point, she didn't look her age. People often told Mary that she didn't either, but her long, auburn hair had many more gray streaks, than it used to. It was her body that made Mary feel so much older, with its aches and pains. Perhaps it was due to raising two children, while Suzie had jetted around as an investigative journalist. However, she wouldn't have traded her role as a mother for anything, she adored her two children, even though the marriage to their father fell apart.

"You know, just because we have two cars, doesn't mean we can't still travel together as often as we like." Suzie looked over at her with a warm smile. "I like our chats on the road."

"Me, too." Mary returned her smile. She considered herself incredibly lucky for sharing a business with her best friend, and living in a town as quaint and beautiful as Garber. As they drove through town she noticed several familiar faces who waved at them. She waved back and smiled. In Garber, everyone got to know everyone. At first that was a little unsettling for Mary, but soon it became quite a comfort.

"The SUV is parked over near the library. It's Kenny from the grocery store selling it. I don't know too much about it, but I'm sure he would give us a good deal." Mary glanced at the digital clock on the dash. Whenever there were new guests coming in she always felt a little anxious. "Maybe we can get all of this settled this morning."

"We'll see, we have to make sure he's not selling us a lemon." Suzie quirked a brow as she turned into the parking lot. She'd had a bit more exposure to dishonest people than Mary had. "That does look pretty nice." She parked beside the silver SUV which had a sign posted in the passenger window. "Let's take a look."

The pair got out of the car and walked around the SUV, peering in windows, and checking the body for dents and rust. They read over the sign in the window that had the details of the SUV and the sale price.

"It looks like it's in good shape." Mary squinted as some early sunlight reflected off one of the mirrors. "Shall I give him a call?"

"Yes, please do. The mileage is great, and the price seems too good to be true." Suzie crossed her arms and met Mary's eyes. "I'd like to find out why that is."

"Let's see what he has to say." Mary dialed the number, and after the first ring, was greeted by an enthusiastic voice.

"Good morning, this is Kenny."

"Hi Kenny, it's Mary, from Dune House." She glanced at Suzie. Suzie gave her a thumbs up and smiled.

"Oh Mary, it's nice to hear from you. What can I do for you?"

"Suzie and I are here looking at the SUV you have for sale, and we wondered if you could tell us a bit more about it."

"Sure, I can do you one better, I'll be right over so you can take a test drive." He hung up before she could say another word.

"He's going to meet us here, so we can test drive it." Mary grinned as she hung up the phone, then looked back at the SUV. "I guess he's pretty eager to sell."

"But why is he so eager to sell?" Suzie wagged her finger through the air, then paced around the SUV again. "I wonder if it needs some major work?"

"Well, at the price he's offering we could afford to do a few repairs on it." Mary bit into her bottom lip. She didn't want to admit to Suzie that she was in love with the SUV. It had all the bells and whistles that she appreciated, from electric seats, to adjustable mirrors, and keyless entry. Plus, if she was honest with herself, she loved the color.

"Hi ladies." Kenny jogged up to them, his face flushed and his short, blonde hair spiked in awkward directions.

"Kenny, did you run all the way here?" Suzie looked at him with wide eyes.

"Well, I was out on my run anyway." He shrugged as he paused beside them. "It was perfect timing. So, you two are interested?" He held out the keys. "You can take her for a spin if you'd like. But before you do, I'll be honest with you, she does need some repairs."

"Ah, I see." Suzie crossed her arms and sent a brief look in Mary's direction.

"Nothing major. Just a few hundred dollars worth of work." He dropped the keys in Mary's outstretched hand. "That's why I lowered the price. It's still a steal, I promise you that."

"Well, let's take it for a spin and find out." Suzie opened the passenger side door and peeked inside. "You've done a great job on the interior."

"Thanks, I didn't use it very often. Mostly, just if I needed to pick up a load of supplies somewhere. It's not great on gas mileage, but if you're just using it around town it's a great vehicle." He held open the driver's side door for Mary. "Go on, once you drive it, you'll see."

"Thanks." Mary stepped up into the SUV. Right away she noticed that it was easier to get into than the car. Being higher up also gave her a better view of the road in front of her. She started up the engine.

"No hesitations, no sputtering, that's good."

Suzie nodded as she played with all of the buttons on the radio, then flipped on the AC unit. "Nice, cold air." She nodded and switched it to heat.

Mary drove out of the parking lot. She felt a little tug to the right as she drove.

"It needs an alignment, but that's not too bad." Mary used the wipers, and the turn signals. "Everything seems pretty good."

"Honestly, I think it's great. I think we should take it." Suzie leaned towards her. "Gun the engine, let's see how this baby acts when you open her up."

"Gun it?" Mary shook her head. "I don't think that's such a good idea."

"Oh, just step on it! Go for it! There's no traffic." Suzie laughed as she rolled down the window and gestured to the empty street. "It's not like you're going to get a ticket."

"All right." Mary shot her a worried look, then she stepped on the gas. She wasn't a very confident driver, but as the engine roared to life she felt invigorated by the sound and the speed. That sense of freedom crashed right down when she caught sight of flashing lights in the rearview mirror. "Oh no." She groaned as the siren wailed.

"Oops." Suzie grimaced, then pointed to a nearby parking lot. "Pull in there." She looked over her shoulder towards the patrol car. "Don't worry, I can talk us out of this."

"You're not the one driving!" Mary gulped as she saw the door of the police car swing open. Then she witnessed a familiar man climb out.

"Oh good, it's Jason!" Suzie clapped her hands and laughed. "See, I told you we had nothing to worry about." She waved to her younger cousin through the passenger side window. "Hey, Jason!"

"Suzie?" Jason walked up to the passenger side of the SUV and peered through the window at both women. "I have to say when I saw an SUV charging down the road I didn't expect it to be driven by the two of you!"

"Actually, only Mary was driving." Suzie grinned as she met her cousin's eyes. "We're going to buy this from Kenny. We just wanted to see what it could do."

"In a thirty-five miles per hour zone?" He looked past Suzie, at Mary, with one eyebrow raised. "She talked you into it, didn't she?"

"I'm so sorry, Jason!" Suzie frowned as she shifted in her seat. "There wasn't any traffic, we didn't think it would be too much of an issue. We weren't going that fast."

"It is." He crossed his arms as he looked at both

of them. "You can't be driving through here like this. I know it's a quiet road, but you have to be careful."

"We know, we never drive like this, Jason. But I was only going slightly over the limit. Listen, we're going to buy the SUV. Do you know of any good mechanics that can do some repairs for us?" Mary eyed him for a moment. "Someone that won't cheat us?"

"Graham's in Parish is a good one. I also like Allen's over on Grove Street, but he's closed for a month." Jason knocked lightly on the door. "So, about this ticket."

"Ticket?" Suzie narrowed her eyes. "You can't be serious."

"Great, just great." Mary frowned as she thought of her insurance rate going up. "He's right, Suzie, I do deserve a ticket."

"Oh no, it's not for you, Mary." He winked at her then pulled out his pad. "Suzie here was creating an unsafe environment with her poor advice given to her innocent friend."

"Ha, ha!" Suzie rolled her eyes, then grinned. "I suppose you're going to expect me to see you in court?"

"No, for dinner, tomorrow night. Both of you if

possible. Summer wants us all to have a nice meal together. You can bring Paul and Wes if they're available." He tapped his pen against his pad. "If you agree to it, I suppose I could let you slide on the ticket, just this once."

"How kind." Mary laughed, then shook her head. "You really had me going there, Jason."

"Sorry, Mary, I had to give Suzie a hard time." He flashed her a smile.

"Unfortunately, we have to make dinner for the guests tomorrow." Mary frowned.

"Why don't you join us instead?" Suzie asked.

"Okay, thank you. I have to check with Summer, but it shouldn't be a problem."

"Perfect." Suzie nodded, then waved him off. "Now, we have important business to handle, and you have actual criminals to chase."

"Criminals? What criminals?" He laughed as he stepped back from the SUV. "It's Garber, nothing bad ever happens here."

As Mary drove back out of the parking lot, she was still a little shaken. "It's nice having your cousin on the police force."

"It is, isn't it?" Suzie laughed. "I can't believe he tried to give me a ticket. What a stinker." She shook her head, but couldn't resist a smile.

As they pulled back into the parking lot where Kenny waited for them, they both waved to him.

"So, what do you think?" He looked between them as they stepped out of the car.

"We'll take it." Mary thrust out her hand towards him. "We have a deal."

"Great." Kenny shook her hand and grinned. "I'll give you a list of the repairs that need to be done. Graham's in Parish is a pretty decent place to get the work done."

"Sounds great." Mary glanced at her watch. "I should have enough time to get to the bank, can you have the paperwork ready in about twenty minutes?"

"Sure, no problem. You can pick it up at the grocery store, my shift is about to start."

"Perfect." Mary looked over at Suzie. "The SUV is definitely mine."

"Yours?" Suzie laughed. "What? No fair."

"I might share once in a while." Mary winked at her. "Now, let's get to the bank."

Suzie climbed back into the driver's seat of the car and they headed over to the bank. As they went through the process of setting everything up for the purchase, Mary continued to glance at her watch.

"We're cutting it close." She frowned. "I need to

do a once-over of the rooms before the guests arrive."

"Try not to worry. We'll get the paperwork from Kenny, then drop the SUV off at Graham's, and we'll be back in plenty of time for the guests." Suzie snapped her fingers. "Simple as pie."

"But don't you need to run some errands?" Mary thanked the teller as she received the bank check for the payment.

"Nothing too urgent. I can handle that after all of the guests are set up. We're in this together, remember?" Suzie wrapped her arm around Mary's shoulders.

"Always." Mary smiled.

CHAPTER 2

*M*ary slid the key into the ignition of the SUV and smiled as the engine purred to life. Sure, it needed a little work, but in general it was in good shape.

"You do like driving this, don't you?" Suzie shifted towards her in the passenger seat.

"I do. I don't know why, but I just do." Mary turned on the radio and rolled down the window. "Good tunes, and good friends, what could be better?"

"Not much." Suzie stretched out in her seat and smiled. "All right, I'll meet you at the garage." She climbed out of the SUV and back into the car.

Mary led the way out of the parking lot and towards the neighboring town of Parish. The GPS on her phone announced the directions to Graham's Garage.

"Here it is," Mary said to herself as she turned into a small parking lot off to the side of a white garage. Other than the large garage doors there was only one other door, with a sign that declared it the office. She stepped out of the SUV just as Suzie pulled into the parking lot behind her. She stepped out of the car and joined Mary.

"It looks like a decent place, hopefully he has time to fix it up today. The sooner the better." Suzie approached the office door. Mary followed after her, but before she could reach the door, a voice called out from inside the garage.

"Can I help you?"

Mary turned on her heel and faced the man who stepped outside. He looked to be in his fifties or sixties with a mane of black and silver hair, as well as a chest-length beard that was just as bushy. He wiped his hands on an already stained, blue cloth that matched the coveralls that stretched across his rounded stomach.

"We're looking for Graham." Suzie shielded her eyes from the sun and peered at the man. "Are you Graham?"

"Depends who is asking." He grinned, and his blue eyes danced in the sunlight.

"Customers." Mary offered him a smile as she held her hand out to him. There was something about him that she instantly liked. "I'm Mary, and this is my friend, Suzie. You were recommended to us for some repairs we need to have done on our new vehicle."

"Ah, great to meet you." Graham clasped her hand with his and gave it a firm shake. "What did you bring me?" He looked past them at the SUV.

"I have a list of repairs that the previous owner said needed to be done. But I'd like you to check it over as well to see if there is anything else wrong." Mary pulled the list out of her purse, along with the keys. "It seems to be running well."

"Good." Graham took the list and the keys from her. "I'll have a good look around. It's a nice vehicle. Congratulations on your purchase. You can head into the office and my secretary will write up a work order for you."

"About how long do you think it will take?" Suzie asked him just before he walked towards the SUV.

"Well now, that's hard to say since I haven't looked at it, yet." He glanced over the list in his hand. "I'll need at least a day, maybe two. Are you in a rush?"

"No, that's fine." Mary smiled. "I'll make sure to leave my number, so you can let me know an estimate on the repairs?"

"Sure, I can do that. If it costs more than what is listed on here I will make sure I get your approval first. Is that okay?"

"Sure." Mary smiled.

"Great." He nodded to them both. "Nice to meet you, ladies." He turned back towards the garage. "Brody! Come get these keys."

A young man in grease-smudged coveralls walked out of the garage, and caught the keys that Graham tossed to him.

"I'm in the middle of something." Brody frowned.

"And now you're pulling that SUV around." Graham pointed to the vehicle. "With a smile, right?"

"Right." He stared at Graham for a long moment, then walked over to the SUV. Suzie pulled open the door to the office, then held it open for Mary. They both barely fit inside. There was a desk, piles of paperwork, an old television, and a few filing cabinets. Aside from that, there wasn't even room for chairs in front of the desk. A petite woman sat behind the desk, and Mary wondered if perhaps Graham had hired her based on how well she would fit into the office. She looked young, perhaps in her twenties, and had ear buds in her ears.

"Excuse me?" Suzie knocked lightly on a tiny, clear space on the desk.

The woman jumped, pulled out her ear buds, and looked up at them with wide, light brown eyes.

"Oh, I'm sorry. How can I help you?"

Mary filled her in on their purpose for being there, and the young woman began to fill out the necessary paperwork.

"Please make a note that we'd like him to call us as soon as he has an idea of the price and when the repairs will be complete." Suzie peered at the woman's name tag. "Carlene?"

"Yes, I will." She smiled. "It's funny isn't it? Yes, people do call me Car, and I work in an auto shop."

"That's cute." Mary grinned.

"Thanks." Carlene finished the last of the paperwork, then gave Mary a copy. "I'll be in touch as soon as we get an idea of what's going on with the SUV."

"Thank you!" Mary nodded.

As they headed back to the car, Suzie glanced over at her.

"Are you sure this is the best place?"

"It was recommended, and he seems nice enough." Mary shrugged.

Suzie was about to open the passenger side door when a bright yellow sportscar roared into the parking lot. The driver jumped out and stalked towards the open garage doors.

"Graham!" He shouted so loudly that Suzie froze where she stood. "Graham!"

The two women exchanged a brief look of concern, then headed back towards the garage. Whatever the man was upset about, it seemed serious.

"Brennan, what are you doing here?" Graham met him at the garage door.

"You know what I'm doing here! I lost every-thing last night, the brakes were faulty!" He took a step towards Graham. "You're going to pay for my car, and more, because I lost a lot last night."

"Calm down, Brennan. We can discuss this." He glanced over at Suzie and Mary and waved his hand. "Don't worry, ladies, I'll have it ready for you soon."

Suzie steered Mary back towards the car.

"We'd better not get into the middle of that."

"If he's upset about the repairs that Graham did on his car, don't you think we should find out why?" Mary glanced over her shoulder at the two men, who disappeared into the garage.

"Not necessarily. We don't know what actually happened to his car. I think with Jason's recommendation, and Kenny's, Graham is still our best bet." Suzie opened the door to the car. "Now, we're on a schedule, remember?"

"I remember." Mary glanced at her watch, then looked back at the garage. The amount of anger she'd seen in Brennan's expression concerned her. But Suzie was right. It wasn't her business, and there was a lot to get done before the guests arrived. She joined Suzie in the car. "Oh, we still need to get tomatoes!"

"Right, let's head that way now before we forget again." Suzie turned into the grocery store just across the border between Parish and Garber. As Mary selected the tomatoes, Suzie browsed through the cleaning supplies to pick up a few products they needed. As she tossed some in her basket she heard a familiar voice, and smiled at the sound of it.

"Summer." Suzie stepped around the side of the aisle and found her cousin's wife at the deli counter.

"Suzie!" She opened her arms for a quick hug. "What are you up to today?"

"Well. We just bought a car." Suzie laughed. "A SUV."

"Wow!"

"I know, a bit impulsive, but it was a great deal."

"Congratulations!" Summer grinned.

"Thanks. We have some new guests coming in, so we're just picking up a few things." Suzie smiled. "Are you off today?"

"I'm training a new assistant. I'm trying not to micromanage, so I took a break." Summer lowered her voice and leaned closer. "It's not an easy thing to let someone else do my job."

"I bet it isn't, because you're the best medical examiner ever." She winked at her.

"Oh, I think you might be a little partial." Summer grinned. "Where's Mary?"

"In produce, picking out tomatoes. We ran into Jason before and we were hoping you would join us for dinner tomorrow night instead of us coming to you, we're hosting it for our guests. I suppose you could bring Jason, too." Suzie laughed.

"I'll double-check with him, but we should be able to do that. See you then, Suzie."

"Absolutely, I'll make sure we have wine." Suzie

gave her a quick wave, then headed off to find the wine. Once she did, she caught up with Mary in produce. She smiled at the sight of her friend sniffing tomatoes. "Did you find some good ones?"

"Yes, I think so." Mary grinned.

"I just invited Summer to dinner tomorrow night." She followed Mary to the checkout aisle.

"That's great." Mary took a deep breath, then smiled. "We really did it, Suzie, we have our very own SUV."

"Yes, we do." Suzie set the bottle of wine on the conveyor belt. "And we're going to celebrate!"

"I sure hope we left the car in good hands." Mary gazed out the window as Suzie drove in the direction of Dune House.

"Me, too. I'm sure he'll do a good job. Someone always has something to complain about, right?" Suzie shrugged as she turned down the road that would lead them home. "The important thing is, we made our purchase. It's getting fixed up, and that's a good reason to celebrate. Right?"

"Right." Mary grinned as they pulled into the parking lot of Dune House. "We only have about an hour before the guests are due to arrive, so I need to get to work on lunch." She grabbed the bag of tomatoes from the back seat. As she climbed out of the car she noticed the sunlight as it glistened on the outstretched ocean. She took a deep breath of the salty air. It was hard to believe that she lived in paradise, but that's what she considered Garber, and Dune House.

"I'll look over the rooms one last time to be sure everything is in place. How many guests are coming in today?" Suzie tucked the keys into her pocket as she approached the front porch.

"Three, a couple, and a young woman on her own. She's only staying one night, the couple will be here through the weekend." Mary followed her up the stairs.

"Oh, that's nice. I like it when the guests stay a bit longer, it gives us a chance to get to know them better." Suzie smiled as she held the door open for Mary.

"I like it, too. I am hosting lunch today. They are on their own for dinner as they all indicated that they wouldn't be in for dinner when I asked them. But tomorrow night I planned to have an early dinner before Anna, the young woman, checks out. Summer, Jason and Wes will hopefully be joining us. I know that Paul will be back tonight so if he wants to join us for dinner that would be great."

"I'll ask. Sometimes he needs a day or two to

settle back in to being on land." Suzie laughed. "I'll let Pilot in, then check on the rooms." She headed back out towards the fenced-in yard.

Mary set the tomatoes down on the counter in the kitchen, then got to work on preparing lunch. It was hard for her to believe that she'd actually purchased a vehicle since she didn't come home with it. Times had certainly changed. There was a time in her life when every decision she made had to be run by her husband, and he tended to be in charge of every choice. It had taken a little time for her to get used to making her own decisions. Suzie helped her adjust to that.

Once the sandwiches were made, Mary started in on the crackers. As she lined them up on a large tray she felt something cold and wet press against the curve of her ankle.

"Pilot!" She gasped and laughed at the same time. "You startled me."

Pilot looked up at her and yawned as he wagged his tail. She reached down and stroked the top of his head.

"Have you been sleeping again, you lazy dog. You'd better be nice to our guests, they'll be here soon."

Pilot wagged his tail again, then sat, and looked up at her with wide eyes.

"Oh, it's a cracker you're after?" Mary clucked her tongue. Then she snatched a cracker off the tray and tossed it to him. He snapped it out of the air. "Don't tell Suzie." She winked at him. She washed her hands, then returned to the task of preparing the lunch spread. Pilot trotted off to look for Suzie, Mary guessed. Ever since they'd adopted him, he'd become as much a part of Dune House as they were. He was quite protective of it and had to be taught to stop barking when a new guest arrived and not to bark every time a guest returned to the property. At first, they'd been concerned that it would be a problem to have a dog at a bed and breakfast, but their guests were informed before they booked, and none had complained. In fact, many spent more time playing with Pilot than they did on the beach. She couldn't blame them, Pilot had an eagerness and joy that was infectious.

When there was a light knock on the door, Mary wiped her hands on her apron and headed towards it. Sometimes guests arrived early. She opened the door and discovered a young couple, their hands clutched together, and excited smiles on their faces.

"Welcome, Jess and Kyle?" Mary smiled.

"Yes, sorry we're a little early, we made better time than we expected." Kyle adjusted the bag that hung from his shoulder.

"That's no problem at all. Come on inside." Mary noticed they didn't have very many bags. "Do you have more luggage in the car?"

"No, we make it our mission to travel light." Jess grinned.

"That is a good thing to do!" Mary smiled as she led them towards the dining room. "I've put out a nice lunch spread if you're hungry. There is plenty. I also put some brochures together of places in town that you might want to visit and there are some coupons in there, and of course we have all of the supplies you may need to enjoy some time on the beach."

"That's great, thanks." Kyle set the bag down on the floor not far from the door. "I'm starving."

"I wouldn't let him stop on the way." Jess laughed as she patted her husband's shoulder. "I was so excited to get here. I can't wait to get on that beach, it looks so beautiful."

"Oh it is, trust me." Mary headed for the kitchen. "What can I get you to drink? We have lemonade, iced tea, bottled water—"

"Oh, who's this? You must be the resident dog."

Kyle laughed as he reached down to pet Pilot. "Hi buddy, aren't you the sweetest?"

"That's Pilot, he's our permanent guest." Mary grinned as she looked back at them. "He's a very friendly dog, but if he gives you any trouble just let me know."

"I'm sure he won't." Kyle straightened up. "I'll take some iced tea."

"Just water for me, thanks."

As they settled in to feast, Mary filled out their paperwork. Just as she finished, there was another knock on the door. She headed for it and opened it to find a man on the other side. He looked to be in his thirties, and his dark hair was held back in a tight ponytail. His brown eyes sought hers.

"Hi there."

"Hi." Mary stared at him and wondered if she had forgotten a guest. As far as she knew it was only the couple, and a young woman who hadn't arrived yet. He certainly didn't fit the description of a young woman. "How can I help you?"

"I'm looking for a place to stay." He cleared his throat. "I heard you might have a room available."

"Oh, I'm so sorry." Mary laughed, then shook her head. "I was confused for a moment there. We usually take reservations in advance, but we do have a room available. I'll just need you to fill out some paperwork. How long do you intend to stay?"

"I'm not sure, yet. A few days, maybe a week." He raised an eyebrow. "Is that possible?"

"Sure, we can leave it open-ended for now." Mary shared with him the nightly and weekly rates, then led him inside to fill out the paperwork. As she settled him in the living room with the forms to fill out, the next guest arrived.

"Welcome, Anna." Mary smiled at her as she ushered her through the door. She had quite a few bags despite only being an overnight guest. She wore very colorful clothing and lots of gold jewelry that nearly matched her long, blonde hair. Mary felt a little overwhelmed as she attempted to monitor the dining guests, the stranger filling out paperwork, and the newest arrival.

Suzie came back downstairs just in time to help Mary in the whirlwind of activity. She leaned in close to Mary.

"Who is in the living room?"

"Actually, I don't know his name, yet. But he needed a place to stay."

"I'll check him in." Suzie stepped into the living room and held out her hand to the man perched on the couch. He looked to be in his twenties, but there was a sense of maturity about him that made her doubt her guess. "Hi, I'm Suzie."

"Hi Suzie." He stood up and shook her hand. "I'm James."

"Welcome to Dune House, James." She held his gaze for a long moment. When he handed her the paperwork, she took it to the front desk and immediately entered the information. She wasn't sure why exactly, but something about James didn't seem all that friendly.

CHAPTER 3

*O*nce all the guests were settled in, Mary guided Pilot outside for a quick run on the beach. She found the young dog behaved much better if he had a good amount of exercise, and she needed it as well. As she thought of seeing Wes at dinner that evening, her heart skipped a beat. She still felt a little silly for being so wrapped up in him. Hopefully, he didn't know just how much she enjoyed his company, or he might think she was a bit foolish. Nothing about Wes made her feel as if he would ever be anything but kind to her, and yet the insecurities from her previous marriage still surfaced to make her wonder.

As Pilot chased a seagull down the beach she laughed and reveled in the warmth of the sun.

When she returned to the house she checked on all the guests, then prepared for her dinner with Wes. Not long after, she heard his familiar knock at the door. Two heavy thumps, and a patter of lighter knocks. It always amused her that he stuck to that pattern. She wasn't sure that he was even aware of it. But it let her know exactly who was outside. The door was unlocked, but he liked to announce his presence, so he didn't startle Suzie or Mary. As Mary headed for the door she noticed James on the side porch. He sat in a chair with his back to the dining room windows, his gaze towards the water. She always liked to see the guests of Dune House enjoying the beauty that Garber had to offer. As she approached the door it flung open and she smiled at the sight of Wes.

"You look so handsome." Mary grinned.

"Well, I do try." He took off his cowboy hat and smiled. "I have to, with someone as beautiful as you on my arm."

"Sure, sure." Mary laughed as she waved her hand at him. It still made her blush when he complimented her. "Enough with the sweet talk, let's go eat."

He smiled and then led her out to his car.

On the short drive to the local diner, Mary filled him in about the newest guests.

"James, I'm not sure about, but I'm sure he'll be fine."

"You can always call me if you're worried about something." He glanced over at her. "You know that, right?"

"Wes, I know I can, but I don't have anything to worry about. I know you would help me in any way that you can, even though I know you have your hands full with all the thefts in Parish at the moment." Mary leaned close to him as he turned into the parking lot of the diner. "But thank you, I know I can call you if I need anything."

"Always." He caught her eye, then focused on finding a parking spot.

As they settled at their favorite table in the diner, Mary shifted nervously in her chair. She wasn't sure if he would approve of her impulsive decision. She didn't necessarily need his approval, but she also didn't want to face his rejection.

"So, I bought a car today." Mary smiled as she folded her hands on the table between them.

"Wait, you bought a car?" He raised his eyebrows as he looked across the table at her. "Or do you mean you're shopping around for one?"

"No, I bought one. Just today." She grinned. "Honestly, I don't believe it myself. I guess I'd believe it more if I was actually driving it."

"Why aren't you driving it?" Wes smiled as the waitress approached. "Let's order first, then you can tell me all about it."

Mary had a hard time picking out what she wanted as her stomach fluttered. Would Wes think she was foolish for not taking more time to make the decision. It wasn't like her to be so impulsive. But that didn't change the fact that she thought she made the right decision. When he looked back at her, she caught sight of a subtle glint in his eyes.

"I can't believe you did that. I'm so impressed."

"Impressed?" Mary looked at him with surprise.

"Yes, very. It's difficult for me to make a decision sometimes. I think working as a detective I'm constantly looking at all the angles, and I'm always looking for what might be hiding behind the scenes. So, even when I know what I want to do, it's hard for me to really go for it. You knew what you wanted and went right for it. That's pretty amazing, if you ask me."

"Well, thanks." She felt her cheeks grow hot as she looked down at the table, then swiftly back up at him. "It's an SUV. Suzie and I thought it would be nice to have to use for guests and for hauling."

"That's a good idea. It's always good to have a larger vehicle around, you never know when you might need it. So, why aren't you driving it?" Wes reached his hand across the table and stretched his fingers out towards her.

"We dropped it off at Graham's in Parish." Mary settled her hand in his and smiled as the warmth of his skin enveloped hers. "It needs a few repairs. Not much, but it's best to just get it done. Do you know the place?"

"Oh sure, Graham has been in business for years. I'm sure he'll do a great job for you." Wes drew his hand back as the food was delivered to the table. "Thanks so much."

"Oh good, I'm so glad to hear that." Mary sighed with relief. "I honestly was a little nervous after leaving it there, because a customer came in shouting at him as we were leaving."

"There are always going to be unhappy customers, but all I've heard about Graham are good things." He picked up his glass of water and held it in the air. "To your new vehicle. Congratulations, Mary!"

"Thanks, Wes!" She smiled as she touched her glass to his.

After dinner, Wes drove Mary back to Dune House and walked her up to the front door. She caught sight of the young couple on the side deck, snuggled together in one of the lounge chairs.

"Thanks for joining me for dinner, Mary."

"Thanks for inviting me." She gave him a quick hug. "Have a good day, tomorrow."

"You, too. You'll have to take me for a ride." Wes winked at her, then walked away.

❧

The next morning Mary woke with a sense of excitement. The buzz of energy pushed her right out of bed, even earlier than usual.

She stretched her arms above her head and yawned. She liked getting up first thing in the morning. It gave her a few minutes of quiet before the day started, and also gave her some time to become fully awake.

Mary said hello to Pilot who was asleep at the foot of her bed. She kept meaning to make him sleep in his basket, but she just couldn't get herself to. She said it was to keep him company, but actually it was to keep her company more than anything else. After getting ready she called Pilot to her side. She bent down to pat his head and he wagged his tail in excitement. She led Pilot outside for a short walk.

As Mary walked along enjoying the beautiful sunrise, she mulled through her experiences the day before. Top on her mind was the SUV. She wondered if it might be ready. After she called Pilot back to her side she walked back towards the house. The gentle lapping of the waves and the sand sifting through her toes helped her to relax and focus on the day ahead. With Pilot by her side she mounted the wooden steps to the back porch and at the top slid her feet into her sandals. As she approached the door she saw that Suzie was already up and making them both coffee in the kitchen.

"Morning Suzie." She smiled as she pushed open the door.

"Morning Mary, how was your walk?" Suzie poured coffee into a mug and handed it to her.

"Great." Mary took the mug and blew across the hot liquid. "Thanks so much for this."

"You're more than welcome." Suzie took in the aroma of her coffee and smiled. "I'm so glad that Paul is back on land. It's nice to think that I can go visit him any time I like."

"How did his trip go?" Mary leaned back against the counter, then took a sip of her coffee.

"He says well, he seems a bit tired. He hit some rough weather. But after a good night's rest he should be okay."

"I'm sure he's glad to be home." Mary tried to distract herself from thoughts about the car, but as the time went by and she still hadn't received a call, she began to get impatient. "I'm going to give Graham a call and see if there's an update on when the car will be ready. They should at least be able to tell us that, right?" She pulled out her phone.

"I would think by now, yes." Suzie glanced at the clock that hung on the wall in the kitchen. "Do you want me to handle breakfast this morning?"

"Would you mind? I just know I'm not going to be able to relax until I find out what's going on at the garage." Mary skimmed through her contacts for the garage's phone number.

"Sure, no problem." Suzie headed back into the kitchen.

As Mary waited for the call to connect she paced through the living room. Although they cleaned frequently, there were always places to dust, or cushions to straighten. She busied herself with the tasks and waited as the phone rang, and continued to ring. She frowned and wondered if perhaps she had called the wrong number. She hung up, then looked up the number of the garage on the internet. She called the number directly from the listing, and again it rang, and rang. There wasn't even an option to leave a message.

Annoyed, she wondered how Graham could have stayed in business so long and had such great recommendations if he never answered the phone. She tucked the phone back in her pocket and decided to focus on the guests for a few minutes, then try to call again. However, as she spoke with them, her thoughts were on the SUV and whether she may have made a mistake. Was Graham not calling because he hadn't even looked at the SUV, yet? Was he not calling because he had looked at it, and it needed so many repairs that he didn't want to tell them? Her stomach twisted as she wondered if she'd made the wrong decision. She placed another call to the garage. After several rings, there was still no answer. Annoyed, she hung up the phone. She knew she wouldn't be able to relax until she had at least an estimate of the cost of repairs, as well as the length of time it would take to make them. She couldn't have that if no one ever picked up the phone.

"I'm going to go over there." Mary grabbed the keys from the counter. "I want to know what's going on. We can always move the SUV to a different mechanic if Graham is not going to work on it."

"Are you sure you want to drive all the way over there?" Suzie frowned. "It's a little strange that no one is answering, but maybe they're not open, yet?"

"It's nearly eleven." Mary glanced at her watch, then back at Suzie. "I'll just feel better if I know exactly what is happening."

"Then you should go." Suzie nodded and glanced out towards the beach. "I'll be around if anyone needs anything."

"Thanks, Suzie!" Mary gave her a quick hug, then headed out the door.

As Mary drove to Graham's, she waited for her cell phone to ring. She expected at any moment that the phone would ring and she would feel incredibly foolish for insisting on driving to Parish. However, her phone didn't ring. When she pulled into the parking lot of the garage, she noticed that the garage doors were open. The office door was closed. She walked towards the garage, annoyed that clearly someone was there, and no one had called her. As she approached she saw a truck in the workspace. Then she saw something that her mind couldn't make sense out of, until a scream emerged from her lips. A pair of legs stuck out from beneath a large truck. It looked as if the jack had given way.

"Hello! Are you okay?" Mary ran forward, and caught sight of Carlene sprawled across the concrete floor a few feet away. Mary dropped to her knees, to peer under the truck. It was clear to her that Graham, who she recognized by his bushy beard, was no longer alive. She forced herself to her feet and rushed to Carlene's side.

As Mary took the woman's pulse she dialed 911 on her phone. She tried to make sense of the scene, however as she relayed what she could to the 911 operator, she had no idea if the information would be helpful. Had the truck somehow fallen on Graham? If that was the case, how did Carlene get knocked out? There was nothing on the ground near her that might indicate she had been hit with a flying object or somehow injured herself. The more she tried to piece it together, the less sense it made, until a shocking realization rippled through her.

"I think someone did this. I think someone hurt them." Mary's heart pounded as she began to look around the garage. Could that person still be nearby?

CHAPTER 4

"Carlene?" Mary shifted closer to her. She gently rubbed her cheeks. "Carlene, can you hear me?"

Mary blinked back tears as the woman remained perfectly still. The operator encouraged her to continue to try to wake her.

"I will. Please send someone soon."

"They're on their way. Can you hear them?"

"Yes." Mary breathed a sigh of relief as sirens wailed in the distance. She hung up with the operator, then focused on Carlene again. As she stroked her hair back away from the nasty bruise on her forehead, Carlene began to stir.

"Stay still, sweetheart, you have quite a bump on your head." Mary held back tears as she tried not to think about Graham under the truck. "Help is on the way, just try to be still."

"I have to help Graham." Carlene's voice was heavy and slurred as she pushed up against Mary's hand that was placed on her arm.

"It's okay, I'm getting him help. Just take a few deep breaths, okay?" She curled her hand around Carlene's and stroked the back of it.

Carlene took a deep breath, but when she took another she began to cough and wince.

"It's okay, take it easy." Mary continued to stroke her hand. "What happened, Carlene? Do you know what happened?"

"I heard Graham scream, and I came in here, and then someone hit me." Carlene reached up and touched the bruise on the curve of her forehead. "And then everything went black."

"Did you see who it was?" Mary looked at the bruise on Carlene's forehead. It stretched across almost half of her forehead.

"No, I just saw a figure, then he hit me." Carlene sniffled as she tried to take another deep breath.

"He?" She looked into Carlene's eyes. "You know it was a man you saw?"

"I'm not sure." She sighed. "I think maybe I just assumed, I can't—" Her voice trailed off.

"It's all right, hon. What about Brody? Where is he? Is he hurt, too?" Mary swept her gaze over the garage for the young mechanic she'd seen the day before.

"No, he's at a class all day." Carlene pushed herself up on her elbows, then groaned.

"Try to be still, everything is going to be fine." Mary patted her hand again, then breathed a sigh of relief as the ambulance pulled up outside the open garage doors, followed by two patrol cars. The paramedics swept Mary away from Carlene. As Mary feared, they did not attempt to treat Graham. As the officers ran into the garage she took a few steps back and surveyed the scene. If someone had intentionally killed Graham, maybe they left a clue behind. As she lingered near the entrance of the garage she ran over in her mind every second she'd experienced since she'd pulled into the parking lot. Had she seen anyone go running? Did she hear an engine start somewhere nearby?

"Mary?" Wes' voice drew her from her thoughts.

"Wes!" She threw her arms around him and held him tight. "Oh, it's so terrible!"

"I know it is, I know." He hugged her for a few seconds, then gently pulled away. "Are you okay? Were you hurt?"

"I'm not hurt. I just came to check on the SUV because no one was answering, and now—"

"It's okay," he said gently. "I have to take a look at the crime scene, just try to stay calm. I'll get someone to bring you some water."

"Oh right, of course." Mary blushed as she realized he was there to work, not just to comfort her. Briefly she had forgotten that he was a detective. As she watched him join the other officers she felt a sense of relief that he was on the case. She was certain that he would be able to get to the bottom of things. But that didn't erase the memory of what she'd seen. She stepped out of the garage and placed a call to Suzie. As she filled her in on what happened, emotions rushed to the surface. What if she had gotten there earlier? What if she had been able to stop it all?

"Mary, sweetheart, I'm so sorry that happened. Come home so we can talk this through."

"I'm not sure I can drive, yet." Mary glanced down at the tremble in her hand.

"Don't worry, I'll drive you. I'll get an officer to pick me up." Wes returned to her side with a small smile. "There's not much more I can do here at the moment. The crime scene techs are going to take over."

"But don't you need to run leads or something like that?" Mary met his eyes.

"I have people working on a few, I can spare a few minutes to drive you home." He wrapped his arm around her shoulders. "Tell Suzie we'll be there soon."

"Wes is going to drive me home, Suzie. We'll be there soon." Mary hung up the phone. Wes led her to her car, and took the keys from her.

"Just relax, tell me what happened as we drive."

Mary shared with Wes every detail that she could recall from the moment that she first started calling the garage that morning until the moment he arrived at the garage.

"I just can't believe this happened. How could anyone do such a terrible thing?"

"We have a possible motive. It looks like some money was taken from the office, but not all of it. So, it might have been a robbery." He slowed down as he entered Garber.

"Someone did this and then didn't even take all the money?" Mary shook her head. "That's pretty senseless. Does that mean it's possible the murderer targeted Graham for personal reasons as well? Maybe the cash was an afterthought?"

"I'm not sure what it means just yet. There is

another possibility." He turned into the parking lot of Dune House.

"What's that?" She glanced over at him as he parked the car.

"It's possible that you interrupted the murderer before they had the chance to get all the cash out of the office." He scratched his cheek, then frowned. "First assessment indicated he'd only been dead a short time before we arrived. An autopsy will have to confirm that."

"I wish that made me feel better, but it doesn't." Mary pressed her hand against her stomach and sighed. "I just keep thinking that if I had been there earlier—"

"Don't." He took her hand in his. "Don't even think that way. If you had been there any earlier, you could have been hurt, or worse. I understand why you feel that way, but Mary, the only thing that would have happened if you were there earlier, is you would have been in a whole lot of danger, and just the thought of that—" He squeezed her hand, then shook his head. "I couldn't stand it if anything ever happened to you."

"That's sweet, Wes." Mary met his eyes, then glanced away as she blushed. "But it doesn't change this feeling I have, that maybe I could have done something."

"I know that feeling all too well." He sighed. "More often than not I walk into a situation when it's too late to prevent harm, but when I get that feeling I remember that it's my task to find whatever justice can be found. That eases the feeling."

"You're right. That's what I should focus on." Mary stepped out of the car.

"Uh, that's not exactly what I meant." Wes stepped out as well. "It's my job to find that justice, remember?"

"And it never hurts to have a sidekick." Mary wrapped her arm around his and winked at him.

"Maybe we should start this conversation over." Wes cleared his throat, but couldn't hide a small smile. He walked beside her up to the front door of Dune House. As he reached for the door to open it, it swung open before he could.

James stood on the other side, his eyes dark, his ponytail a bit messy.

"Excuse me." He brushed past Wes, barely nodded to Mary, then hurried down the front steps.

"Who was that?" Wes turned to look in the man's direction.

"James." Mary watched as the man disappeared along the beach. "Not the friendliest guy."

"I see that." Wes winced as he checked a text on his phone. "I have to run. Mary, will you be okay?"

"Absolutely." She kissed his cheek. "Good luck on the investigation."

"Thanks." Wes met her eyes as if he might say something more, then headed for the waiting patrol car instead.

As Mary stepped inside Dune House, she heard Suzie call out to her as she walked towards her.

"Mary? Is that you?"

"Yes, it's me." She smiled as Suzie hugged her, then pulled away.

"Are you okay?"

"If everyone would stop asking me that, I might be." Mary laughed, then shook her head. "I'm sorry, Suzie, I just don't know how to react. It was horrible, but now all I want to know is who did this, and why?"

"I understand." Suzie led Mary into the living room. "You want to know what happened. But you've still had quite a shock. Does Wes have any suspects?"

"Not yet, I don't think. I did tell Wes about the man we saw at the garage yesterday. The one that argued with Graham. He said he would look into it." Mary settled into her favorite chair and stretched her legs out in front of her, as she released a heavy breath. She gave Pilot a few pats. "I'm sorry I was gone so long this morning. How were things here?"

"Smooth. I put some things together for lunch, but no one has shown up to eat anything. Let me bring you a plate." Suzie headed for the kitchen.

"No Suzie, no thanks. I don't think I can eat right now." Mary winced. "My nerves are shot. I just keep wondering what I could have done to stop it, why is he gone?" Mary wiped at her eyes. "I know I didn't even know him, not really, but still."

"Still, it's a shock to meet someone one day and find them gone the next." Suzie perched on the edge of her chair and leaned close. "It's okay to be upset, Mary. You have every reason to be. But I think the best way to get through this is to put that grief into action."

"What do you mean?" Mary met her friend's eyes.

"I say, we find out what exactly happened in that garage. We already know he had at least one enemy, the man we saw in the garage yesterday. What if we do some searching on him and his business and see if there is anything else we can dig up? It can only help in the investigation. Maybe it will lead to something?" Suzie patted Mary's shoulder. "I'll go grab my computer."

"Yes, I think that would help me feel better." Mary's mind began to race with possibilities. "Do you really think it's possible that someone could get so angry over a car that he would kill?"

"Anything is possible these days!" Suzie waved her hand as she headed to her room to grab her computer.

When Suzie walked past one of the guest rooms she noticed a piece of paper wedged beneath the door at the corner. She reached down and picked it up, as she assumed it was a piece of garbage. However, as she took a closer look she noticed that it was a receipt from Graham's Garage. The item listed on the receipt was a canister of oil. She stared at the receipt for some time as she tried to piece together how it had ended up there. She'd found it wedged in James' door. But as far as she knew James didn't have a car there. Why would he need to buy a canister of oil, and why would he go all the way to Parish to buy it? She tucked the receipt into her pocket just as heavy footfalls began down the hallway. She looked up and into James' eyes. The man stared back at her, as if he was just as startled to find her standing there.

"James."

"Suzie." He nodded to her briefly, then glanced at the door to his room. "I just need to get something from my room."

"Have you decided how long you'll be staying with us, yet?" Suzie stood her ground, which meant he had no access to his room.

"I'm sorry, not yet. It probably won't be much longer, though." James frowned as he studied her. "Do you need an exact day?"

"No, that's fine. I found this on the floor. I thought it was just garbage, but it's a receipt. Does it belong to you?" Suzie held the slip of paper out to him.

"No, it's not mine." James barely glanced at it. "I'm in a bit of a hurry, if you don't mind."

Suzie stared at him again. Words poised on the tip of her tongue. She was certain that the receipt belonged to him, how else would it end up in the crack of his door? No one else had a reason to be anywhere near his room. However, she wasn't sure that pushing the matter at the moment would be the best decision. Instead, she tucked the receipt into her pocket and nodded.

"All right then, enjoy your day." Suzie stepped aside, but glanced back over her shoulder and watched as he entered his room. He barely opened the door wide enough for him to get through, then closed the door behind him again. It seemed clear to Suzie that he was hiding something. She lingered by the door for a moment, then continued on to her room to grab her computer.

CHAPTER 5

hen Suzie returned to the living room with her computer, she found Mary staring out through the window nearest to her. She looked deep in thought.

"Here we go." Suzie pulled a chair over beside Mary and popped open the computer. Then she reached into her pocket and pulled out the receipt. She used the camera on her phone to snap a picture of it.

"What's that?" Mary looked at the slip of paper.

"Take a look at it." Suzie handed it over to her. "I found it in the crack of James' door." She glanced out into the dining room, and towards the stairs that led into the living room for any sign of his presence, then lowered her voice. "I think it's very strange, don't you? He claims it isn't his, but who else could it belong to?"

"It is very strange. And, it looks like he made the purchase yesterday, not long after we dropped off the SUV." Mary tapped her fingertips lightly on her knee. "Why would he need oil if he doesn't have a car?"

"I have no idea. He did show up here right out of the blue." Suzie narrowed her eyes as she looked over the receipt again. "Something isn't adding up here."

"I think you're right." Mary turned her attention to the computer. "Do you think we'll be able to find much about Graham?"

"If the garage had a website then there will be reviews. They might at least give us an idea of the kind of man that Graham was, and who he might have been involved with." After a quick search Suzie ascertained that Graham's Garage did not have a website, but she did find a few posts about the garage on a car racing forum. "I've got something here."

Mary leaned close to take a look.

"You do?"

"Listen." Suzie pointed out one of the posts, then began to read it. "I trusted Graham with my life, and almost lost it because of him. He assured me that he had fixed my braking problem, but when I raced my car tonight the brakes gave out and not only did I practically lose my car, but I could have lost my life, or taken out other drivers with me. Don't trust this man for a second!" She cleared her throat as she glanced at Mary. "Does that sound familiar?"

"The man from the garage yesterday." Mary nodded. "He was so upset. Does it list his name?"

"Better than that, it links his social profile." Suzie clicked the link. "It looks like he's a pretty well-known amateur race car driver." She tipped the computer so that Mary could see a photograph of him clearly. "It looks just like him, doesn't it?"

"Yes. Brennan Coopers." She pursed her lips as she studied the man. He had an arrogant smile on his lips, and his helmet tucked under his arm. "Nothing about him screams killer."

"Maybe not in that photograph, but we were there yesterday, we both heard how angry he was. It sounds like he thought Graham conned him." Suzie brushed a few strands of her hair away from her eyes. "I'm going to do some more searching and see if anything else stands out." She paused, then sat forward in her chair. "Well, isn't this interesting."

"Well?" Mary stared at her friend who remained quiet. "Suzie!" She sighed. "You can't just say something like that, and then not tell me." She shook her head. "What did you find?"

"Sorry, sorry, I was reading." Suzie flashed her a brief smile. "It looks like this particular person posted on a review site that they had quite a problem with customer service. She went into the garage to have a taillight fixed, and had to wait several minutes to even speak to anyone. There was no one present in the garage, despite the sign saying that it was open for business."

"Maybe they were busy with other things?" Mary narrowed her eyes. "Where was Carlene or Brody?"

"That's where the review gets interesting. She said she heard shouting, so she walked to the back of the garage. And Graham was there screaming at Brody. He was very upset and ran out past the woman. Graham then offered to fix the woman's car, but she refused and told him he shouldn't treat his staff that way. She went to look for Brody, but couldn't find him, so she just left." She looked over at Mary. "What kind of boss screams at his staff?"

"Not a very good one." Mary crossed her arms.

"Brody was so upset with Graham. I wonder what they were fighting about?"

"They don't say, and it's anonymous. But it does show that there was some tension at one point between Graham and Brody. If that's the case, then we can't just assume he had no ill will towards him."

"No, we can't, but maybe the person that posted that is exaggerating."

"Yes, I guess you're right, it is a bit of a stretch to go from an argument to murder. The only person that really expressed rage at Graham was Brennan. I think we should pay him a visit and find out more about that." Suzie closed her computer, then checked her watch. "But not today. Today you need to get some rest, put those knees up, and let me wait on you."

"Suzie, that's really not necessary, I'll be fine."

"Nonsense. No arguing with me, Mary, you know better." Suzie patted her friend's shoulder. "I'm going to tidy up the kitchen from lunch, let me know when you're ready to eat something, okay?"

"I will." Mary sighed. She hated to be a burden to Suzie, but she knew she was right. After being on her knees on the concrete floor of the garage, they ached quite a bit. As she relaxed into the chair with Pilot at her feet, she went over her visit to the garage that morning, yet again. She was certain that she missed something.

It wasn't until Mary's cell phone rang and she jerked awake that she realized she had fallen asleep. She grabbed for her phone before it could fall out of her lap. A quick check of the time revealed she'd been dozing for a little over an hour. When she saw the caller was Wes she answered right away.

"Hi Wes." She grimaced when she realized how strange her voice sounded. She wasn't quite awake yet.

"Mary, are you all right? Did I wake you?"

"I'm fine." She cleared her throat. "Sorry. How are you?"

"I thought I'd check in with you. Could I stop by?"

Mary smiled to herself. He was such a gentleman. He usually went out of his way to be sure that he asked before showing up at Dune House, even though she'd told him many times that he was welcome to come anytime.

"Absolutely. I'd love to see you. Suzie and I have some things to discuss with you." She wiped the sleep from her eyes.

"You do? Ah, this should be interesting. I'll be there soon." He hung up the phone.

"Who was that?" Suzie joined her in the living room with Pilot at her side.

"Wes, he's coming to give an update."

"Oh great, I wonder what he will think of what we found?" She sat down across from Mary. "Did you have a nice nap?"

"Yes, thank you. I'm curious about what he might have found out."

The two discussed the murder as they waited for Wes to arrive. When there was a knock on the door, Mary started to stand up, but Suzie jumped to her feet.

"Let me get it."

"All right, thanks."

Suzie walked to the door with a smile as Wes pushed through it.

"Wes, it's good to see you."

"You, too." He followed her into the living room and greeted Pilot who was excited to see him. "Where are your guests?"

"No one is here at the moment. The lovebirds are really enjoying the beach, and our solo guests have been out most of the day." Suzie sat back down across from Mary.

Wes pulled a chair close to both of them. "So, what have you two uncovered?"

"Just that Brennan was quite furious with Graham." Mary slid forward some in her chair.

"That's not surprising. I had an interview with Brennan a little while ago, and while he does seem quite upset about his car, he also didn't strike me as being involved in the crime." He tipped his head from side to side. "It's hard to say right now though, everything is still developing. The medical examiner did confirm that the time of death occurred twenty to thirty minutes before we arrived. I've also been looking into Graham's personal finances and he was having some trouble at the shop."

"Interesting." Suzie tapped one foot on the floor. "Maybe he borrowed money from the wrong person?"

"Maybe. But dead men can't exactly pay off their debts." Mary narrowed her eyes.

"Good point. I'm looking further into the financial issues. He didn't have much family to speak of, so we're still trying to track down who might be considered next of kin."

"Poor fellow." Mary began to cough before she could say anything more.

"Oh, let me get you some water." Wes jumped to his feet before Suzie could stand up. He headed for the kitchen to get the water, but Pilot tried to sneak past him which caused Wes to stumble and strike his head on a shelf that stuck out from the living room wall.

"Ouch!"

"Oh, Wes!" Mary launched to her feet. "Are you okay? I'm so sorry, Pilot gets a little excited sometimes."

"Especially when he thinks it involves food." Suzie stood up as well.

"I'm fine." Wes rubbed the red spot on his forehead. "It's not a big deal."

"Let me get you some ice." Mary pulled his hand away from his forehead and eyed the redness from the bump. "That's going to leave a bruise."

"It's okay." He caught her hand and brought it to his lips for a kiss. "I'll be fine. I'm supposed to be getting you water, remember?"

"You get me water, I'll get you ice." Mary grinned as she led him into the kitchen. She grabbed an ice pack from the freezer and turned back to apply it to his head. She noticed the mark was so much smaller and redder than Carlene's had been. "Was Carlene okay?" Mary asked.

"She'll be fine. It was a nasty bump, though." Wes shifted his head some as the ice pack touched his skin.

"Be still now, we have to get the swelling down."

"I could get used to this kind of treatment." He smiled at her as she pulled the ice pack back.

Mary smiled and placed a light kiss on his forehead.

CHAPTER 6

*A*fter Wes left, Suzie and Mary took Pilot for a walk on the beach to wear him out.

"I don't think Wes is really considering Brennan as a suspect." Mary tossed a treat to Pilot.

"I know. But I still think he should be." As a wave rushed up to her, Suzie dipped her bare toes in the water.

"He has to follow the steps of his investigation."

"But we don't." Suzie glanced over at her. "If Brennan did this, then this is the best time to find out. He's probably still reeling from the attack this morning and he might slip up and make a mistake. I'm sure he rehearsed what he would say to the police, but what if it's not the police asking him questions?"

"What are you suggesting?" Mary called Pilot back to them. He ran straight towards them, kicking up the sand behind him.

"I think we should have our own conversation with Brennan. There's a race this afternoon, we know where he'll be." Suzie met Mary's eyes. "What do you think?"

"Good idea. Let's see what he has to say."

After they returned Pilot to the house, they headed to the racetrack. It was located just outside of Garber, in Parish.

"Ready to make a bet?" Suzie flashed Mary a grin as she pulled the car into the parking lot of the racetrack.

"I don't think it's that kind of racing." Mary shot her a brief smile. "But then again, I guess anyone can bet on anything, can't they?"

"Yes, they can." Suzie parked, then stepped out of the car. With Mary right behind her, she headed through the entrance of the large building that faced the racetrack. The crowd inside was mostly gathered around the tall windows that faced the track, while others were piled up in the stands outside that lined the track.

"Wow, I didn't realize this was such a busy place." Mary glanced around at the people gathered.

She didn't notice any familiar faces, but that didn't surprise her as Parish was a much larger town than Garber, and she wasn't as familiar with the residents there.

"Now, the question is, can we find Brennan?" Suzie skimmed the hallway for any hint of which direction to go in. It didn't take her long to find a sign that indicated that the door would lead to the racetrack itself. She gestured to Mary to follow her and headed for the door. As soon as she opened it she was greeted by noise. She could hear the engines of the race cars revving, and the chatter of the people seated in the stands. Though she wasn't much for races, she couldn't deny the buzz of excitement in the air as she descended metal steps towards the dirt ground. She glanced back at Mary who was a bit slower than her down the steps.

"I'm coming." Mary followed after her friend. She made it to the bottom step, then released a heavy breath. "There's Brennan." She tipped her head towards a small section of the track that was shielded by an overhang from the building. A few men in jumpsuits stood there, one of them was Brennan.

"Let's get to him before the race starts." Suzie grabbed her hand and guided her towards the men.

"But what are we going to say?" Mary frowned as she trailed behind. "Shouldn't we have a plan?"

"Don't worry, I've got this." Suzie cast a wink in her direction, then waved as she approached Brennan.

"Brennan! Is that really you? Oh, I can't believe this! Can you believe this, Mary?" She looked over at Mary with a wide grin, then back at Brennan, who gazed at her with some suspicion.

"No, I can't." Mary replied with feigned enthusiasm. She picked up on Suzie's intentions easily. "It must be our lucky day!"

"It is!" Suzie clapped her hands as she studied the man before her. "I thought maybe we would get a glimpse of you, but to actually get to meet you in person, this is so amazing."

"Looks like you have some fans, Brennan." One of the other men elbowed him and grinned. He gestured to the other two and they walked off together.

"Fans, huh?" Brennan pulled off his hat and scratched the top of his head. "I wasn't aware that I had any fans."

"Are you kidding?" Suzie sighed and placed her hands over her heart. "I just love watching these races, the exhilaration! And you are one of the best, of course."

"Thanks." He studied her. "I'm not used to having such good fans. I doubt that anyone other than my mother could pick me out of a line-up of local drivers."

"We're here to prove you wrong." Mary smiled, then her eyes widened. "Oh, but that terrible crash, I heard about that."

"I was so scared for you." Suzie patted his arm and felt the muscles hidden beneath the strained sleeve of his jumpsuit. "How did you lose control?"

"Oh, the crash." His expression darkened, then his eyes narrowed. "Yes, that was terrible. I had been having some problems with my brakes, and I thought they had been fixed. However, it turned out they weren't. That is the last time I will rely on a mechanic to do any work on my car. From now on, I will do it myself."

"Awful!" Suzie gasped. Relieved that he didn't seem to recognize either of them from the garage, she shifted to a more pointed question. "That mechanic should lose his license. I mean, he almost killed you. Shouldn't he be arrested for that?"

"Oh, I was quite upset." He rubbed his hands together, cast a look towards the track, then back at both of them. "However, he's the one who lost his life."

Suzie's heart skipped a beat as he gazed at her with a hint of malice in his expression.

"What do you mean?" Mary stepped closer to Suzie. "Were you so upset that you hurt him?"

"What?" Brennan chuckled, then shook his head. "No, of course not. But he met his maker, anyway. Someone killed him, and I can't say that he didn't have it coming. It's never okay to murder someone, but as angry as I was at him, I could understand why someone might want to. Anyway, the point is that there is no need to dwell on the crash, or the faulty brakes. I need to just move forward. I've checked over my brakes very well, so today's race should go smoothly. I'm racing a different car today, though, mine still needs to be repaired. You'll have to look for me, number twelve." He tipped his cap to the women. "Wish me luck!"

"Good luck!" Mary waved to him as he walked away.

"Well, that was pretty close to a confession, wasn't it?" Suzie turned to face her.

"It certainly sounded like it." Mary crossed her arms. "He should be on the top of the suspect list.

But if he really did it, would he be bragging about Graham's murder that way? That seems a little strange to me."

"It doesn't seem normal, that's for sure. But it could also mean that he didn't do it, and is not the least bit concerned about being suspected. Perhaps he's already given Wes an alibi." Suzie glanced up at the glass windows that overlooked the racetrack. She froze at the sight of a familiar face.

As Suzie peered through the thick glass she second guessed herself. Was it just her imagination that he looked familiar? Many people looked very similar. But the more she looked, the more certain she became.

"Isn't that James?" She tipped her head in his direction, but didn't point.

"I'm not sure." Mary squinted as she leaned towards the windows, then nodded. "Yes, I think it is."

"What would he be doing here?" Suzie narrowed her eyes.

"Let's go find out." Mary started back up the steps with Suzie right behind her. At the landing she pushed the door open and headed back down the hallway to the main lobby.

"Do you see him?" Suzie caught up with her and searched through the crowd.

"There!" Mary pointed at the windows, where James still stood. While everyone else focused on the race about to take place, his gaze angled in another direction, towards the shaded area.

"What is he looking at?" Suzie stepped closer to her.

"I'm not sure, but I want to find out why he's here at all. He didn't mention anything about being here for the races." Mary started to push through the crowd towards James.

He turned to face her just as she reached him. His eyes widened at the sight of her.

"Mary, what are you doing here?"

"Oh, we're fans." Suzie linked her arm through Mary's as she caught up with her. "We never miss a race."

"Really?" His gaze shifted between the two of them with a furrowed brow.

"Really." Mary crossed her arms. "I didn't realize you were here for the races."

"Ah, yes." He glanced over his shoulder at the windows. "I enjoy them."

"Glad you found something to occupy your time here." Suzie smiled.

"Don't forget about dinner tonight." Mary met his eyes. "I'm making a nice home-cooked meal."

"Right, I don't think I'll be able to make it. Thanks, though." He glanced over his shoulder again, when he looked back at them his expression was grim. "If you'll excuse me, I have some business to tend to." He brushed past the two of them. Instead of watching the race, he headed straight for the exit.

"Stranger, and stranger." Suzie tapped her fingers lightly against her thigh. "Let's follow him."

"I'm with you." Mary matched her pace as they headed out the door. As it swung shut behind them, they were faced with a full, but still parking lot.

"Where is he?" Suzie shielded her eyes as she looked through the parking lot.

"There!" Mary pointed to the only moving vehicle in the parking lot, a yellow taxi that turned out onto the street. "That must be him!"

"Hurry!" Suzie started towards the car, but Mary grabbed her arm before she could get far.

"It's too late. We'll never be able to catch up. Besides, we don't want him to catch us following him." Mary slid her hands into her pockets as she considered the possibilities of how he might be involved. "Right now, all we know is that he likes races."

"And that he buys oil, but travels in taxis." Suzie raised an eyebrow.

"True. But maybe he needed it for something else? Maybe it wasn't his receipt? I say we keep a close eye on him." Mary glanced at her phone. "We have enough time to stop by Carlene's if you want. I'm curious about how she's doing, and she really is the only witness."

"She said that she didn't see anything, though." Suzie crossed her arms.

"She did. But she also said that she was fairly certain the murderer was a man, which means she did see something, perhaps much more than she thought." Mary led her towards the car. "We should pick up some flowers on the way. We'll have to make it a quick stop at Carlene's, because I need to start preparing dinner soon, and Jason might stop by early."

"Is Wes going to be joining us?" Suzie settled in the driver's seat.

"I doubt it. When he's on a case that's what he tends to focus all of his time on until it's solved." Mary buckled her seat belt. "Maybe if he gets a break?"

"I still can't shake the feeling that James is up to something." Suzie steered the car down the road as Mary entered Carlene's address into her phone's GPS.

"Honestly, I'm not sure what to think of him, but that receipt is stuck in my mind." Mary pointed out a turn to Suzie.

"Yes, I agree." Suzie turned, then frowned. "I still don't see a connection between the two of them. However, Brennan, he definitely had a connection."

"I wonder how many of Graham's customers were left that unsatisfied. It surprises me that Kenny, Jason and Wes would recommend him, but Brennan had such a terrible experience with him." Mary pointed out the next turn.

"It's possible that Graham didn't do anything wrong. Maybe Brennan just had a bad race and he needed to blame the damage to his car on someone. From what I have read about him on the internet he is known for being a little wild with his driving." Suzie followed Mary's directions through a few stop signs.

"That's true. We're assuming a lot here. What we absolutely know is that Brennan was upset with Graham about his car. Hopefully, Carlene can tell us more about the man she saw, that may give us a new lead, or confirm that it was Brennan. But why would he rob the place?"

"Opportunity? To cover up the real motive?"

"After this left, the house should be on the right about halfway down the road." Mary pointed out the street to turn on to.

"We can hope, if she's even willing to talk to us." Suzie scanned the houses on the side of the road for Carlene's house.

"I hope she's recovering okay. She had such a bad bump on her head. Oh, there it is!" Mary pointed to a small house.

"Great." Suzie pulled into the driveway. She noticed there was a car parked there. "It looks like we caught her at home."

"Just keep in mind that she's been through a very traumatic experience. She may not be able to remember anything, and us asking her questions might make it even harder."

"You're right. We need to be delicate about this." Suzie stepped out of the car.

"I wouldn't want to cause her any more pain." Mary hesitated at the top of the driveway. "Maybe this wasn't such a good idea."

"It'll be okay." Suzie patted her shoulder. "I

want to see how she's doing, and this is the best time to find out any information she might know."

"Okay, deep breath." Mary took a deep breath, then headed up the driveway with Suzie right behind her.

CHAPTER 7

*A*lthough Carlene's house was small, the details of its architecture drew Suzie's attention.

"Cute place." Suzie swept her gaze over the arched windows.

"Neat, too." Mary eyed the garden on either side of the front walkway. "Carlene must be a good gardener."

"I'm sure she'll still appreciate the flowers." Suzie held up the bouquet as Mary knocked on the door.

A moment later the door swung open, and Carlene stood before both of them. The bruise on her forehead was just as daunting as it had been the day before.

"Hi Carlene." Mary held her hand out to her. "How are you holding up?"

"I'm okay, I guess." Carlene took her hand with a brief squeeze, then accepted the flowers from Suzie. "Thank you for these. They will really brighten up the place." She stepped back some. "Would you like to come in?"

"Thanks." Mary stepped into the house, but as she did her foot caught on a boot beside the door. Her knee twisted and gave out. She just managed to grab the door frame before she would have fallen to the floor.

"Oh no, I'm sorry about that." Carlene kicked the boots out of the way. "Are you okay?"

"Yes, it's just my knees. Nothing to be sorry about." Mary frowned as her face flushed with embarrassment.

"Do you need to sit down, Mary?" Suzie gently grasped her arm to make sure she was steady on her feet.

"I'm fine, thanks." Mary waved her away and gave her a brief smile. "Sorry for the strange entrance, Carlene. We came here to check on you."

"I'm as well as I can be." Carlene led them into her small living room. She perched on an overstuffed chair, which left a threadbare couch for Suzie and Mary to share. "I just can't stop thinking about Graham. I keep asking myself, was there something more I could have done?"

"I understand that." Mary sat down on the couch then leaned across to place her hand on Carlene's knee. "I feel the same way. Maybe if I had showed up a little earlier, I could have done something."

"Then you do understand." Carlene placed her hand over Mary's. "But Graham and I had worked together for so long, we'd become like family. It's hard for me to believe that he's gone."

"I'm so sorry for your loss." Suzie crossed one leg over the other. She passed a quick look in Mary's direction, then looked back at Carlene. "I've worked for a lot of different people, and I have to say, I've never had that tight-knit relationship with any. In fact, I often butted heads with them. He must have been someone very special for you two to get along so well, or maybe you are the special one."

"Me?" Carlene laughed a little, then shook her head. "No, there's not much special about me. But Graham, he just had a way of making me feel comfortable. He always treated me with respect, and you're right, that kind of relationship is extremely hard to come by. I considered myself very lucky to have it."

"And you were." Mary settled back against the couch and smiled. "But I'm sure there must have been moments here and there that you didn't agree. It's funny how things seem like such a big deal at the time, but then something like this happens, and it just makes you realize that whatever the issues were, they just don't matter anymore."

"Exactly." Carlene sighed as her eyes fell shut. "The little things here and there can add up, but now, it's nothing. Now, I would trade just about anything to get Graham back."

"Again, I'm so sorry." Mary frowned. "Did Graham have a lot of family?"

"No, not at all. His wife died years ago, and they never had any children. If he had any siblings, he never mentioned them to me. He did have a lot of friends in the community, though. Mostly people he would work on cars for, give them great discounts, that kind of thing. I have no idea who will even plan his funeral. Do you think I should do that?" She grabbed a tissue from the tissue box beside her and dabbed at her eyes. "I wouldn't even know where to begin."

"I'd say wait, the police will try to locate any extended family that Graham may have had. Maybe they will find someone." Suzie winced as the woman began to cry. "I know this is such a delicate thing to talk about."

"What about the garage? What about all of the cars waiting for repairs? I suppose I will have to call and inform all of the customers." Carlene ran her hands back through her hair. "There's just so much to do."

"Do you have anyone to help you?" Mary scooted forward on the couch and looked into the young woman's eyes. "A boyfriend or a friend? Can't Brody help out? This is a lot to have on your shoulders."

"No, Brody already has another job. He won't help me if he isn't going to get paid for it. I don't have anyone." Carlene sighed again, then grabbed another tissue. "I guess Graham and I were alike that way. But you're right, I should take this one step at a time. I can't tell you how much I appreciate your visit, but now I'm starting to feel pretty tired."

"Of course, you are." Suzie nodded and stood up from the couch. "I hope you're able to get some rest. But I want you to know that Mary and I are available to you, should you need anything." She handed her a business card. "Anything at all."

"Thanks." Carlene stood up as she took the card from Suzie. "I will keep in touch."

"Graham seemed like such a nice man." Mary smiled some. "I wish we had the chance to get to know him better."

"You would have liked him." Carlene smiled. "He was such a respectful man, one of the best that I've worked for." She stood up. "I really should try to get some rest."

"Yes, of course." Mary nodded.

The two women headed for the front door. They were silent as they walked to the car. Suzie settled in the driver's seat. Mary took the passenger side, and stared out through the windshield as Suzie reversed out into the street.

"That was an interesting fairytale." Suzie shifted the car into drive.

"Do you think so?" Mary looked out through the window at the house as the car began to roll past it. "She seemed pretty upset."

"Yes, she did. But don't forget about that post we read. Things were not as rosy as she described. At least not all the time. It appears as if Graham definitely had some problems with his staff. I guess maybe he was different to her, and sometimes people do become fonder of someone after they have passed away." Suzie tilted her head back and forth. "It's possible that she's just trying to hide whatever problems they may have had because she doesn't want it to look bad in the investigation."

"Even if Graham was bad to his staff and even if she really did have a terrible relationship with him, that doesn't mean she had anything to do with the murder." Mary licked her lips, then clenched her jaw. "But she is lying about something."

"More than one thing I think." Suzie laughed. "But what do you mean?"

"She doesn't live alone, and I think she definitely has a boyfriend."

"How do you know that?" Suzie turned off the side street.

"Those boots I tripped over, weren't her size. They were large enough to be men's. As far as I know most men don't leave their boots behind unless they are living there." Mary looked over at Suzie. "Wouldn't you agree?"

"Yes, I would." Suzie narrowed her eyes. "I didn't even notice that. Good eye, Mary."

"It's hard not to notice when you almost fall on your face." Mary smiled briefly. "So, who is the mystery man she is living with, and why is she lying about him?"

"Very good questions." Suzie drummed her fingertips on the steering wheel. "We definitely need to find out the answers."

CHAPTER 8

*M*ary drained the water from the pot, then swirled the remaining pasta around to be sure that it was sufficiently drained. As she began to add the sauce, she heard a voice behind her.

"Mary, what have I told you about that sauce?" Jason took a deep breath of the aroma. "It should be illegal for something to smell that good."

"But it's not yet." She grinned as she turned to face him. "So, no arresting me."

"For now." He narrowed his eyes and patted his hip, where his handcuffs hung.

"Who are you threatening to arrest, now?" Summer laughed as she walked into the house behind him. "Oh, it's the sauce, isn't it?" She grinned as she wrapped her arms around Jason's waist. "You are going to have to teach me how to make that, Mary. I've tried, and every time he says it's not quite right."

"Jason!" Mary waved a spoon in his direction. "That is no way to treat your wife."

"I always tell her it's good!" He held up his hands in surrender. "It's just not quite the same."

"He's right." Summer released him and joined Mary near the stove. "He is quite polite about it."

"Don't worry, we'll have a sauce session soon." Mary smiled and leaned over to hug Summer. "But I'm sure your sauce is delicious. Suzie will be back in a few minutes. She just walked down to the docks to see if Paul will be joining us."

"How are you holding up?" Summer rested her hand on Mary's shoulder. "After what happened?"

"I'm doing all right." Mary bit into her bottom lip. "I just want the murderer found quickly."

"They will be, I'm sure." Summer met her eyes.

"Let's not dwell on that." Mary wiped her hands on her apron, then smiled. "Tonight, we are going to enjoy a nice dinner together, and that is what matters."

"Yes, it is." Jason glanced over the kitchen. "Do you need any help with anything?"

"Actually, if you could get down the glasses for me that would be great. They're in the cabinet above the refrigerator."

"On it." He nodded and walked over to the cabinet. As he handed the glasses down to Summer, he glanced over at Mary again. "I did a background check on James."

"You did?" Mary turned her attention towards him.

"Yes, I was a bit suspicious of him turning up out of the blue." Jason nodded. "I wanted to make sure you were safe."

"Did anything pop up?"

"Nothing. In fact, so much nothing, that it makes me suspicious." He handed the last glass to Summer.

"I'll put these on the table." She walked out to the dining room, as the front door opened. Suzie and Paul stepped inside.

"Summer!" Suzie smiled when she saw her. "I'm so glad you could join us tonight."

"Me, too. That new assistant is working out great so far."

"Good to see you, Summer." Paul nodded to her as he hung up his jacket on the coat rack near the door. "Is Jason here?"

"In the kitchen with Mary. They're talking shop." Summer rolled her eyes, then laughed.

"I'd better get in there then." Suzie grinned. "Oh Paul, will you open up that bottle of wine for me?" She pointed to the wine on the table.

"Sure, no problem."

Suzie stepped into the kitchen as Jason stepped closer to Mary and lowered his voice.

"The thing is, for someone's record to be that clean, it can mean two things. Either the guy is a model citizen who has never parked in the wrong place or sped, or he's a lie." He glanced at Suzie as she entered the kitchen. "Hey Suzie."

"Hey Jason." Suzie looked between them. "What's this about?

"James." Jason looked at Suzie. "I did a background check on him because of the murder, and you said he just turned up out of the blue."

"And?" Suzie asked.

"His background is flawless." Jason crossed his arms.

"That's just hard for me to believe. Something about him just seems so off." Mary shook her head.

"I agree." Jason glanced over his shoulder as the young couple arrived for dinner, then looked back at them. "I'm going to look into it more, but for now, exercise caution around him. All right? Let me know if you notice anything strange."

"Okay, we will." Suzie frowned as Jason walked back out into the dining room to introduce himself to the guests. "That's a bit concerning."

"Yes, it is. Maybe his real reason for being here has nothing to do with car races." Mary finished putting together the pasta. "You did find that receipt. Remember?"

"Yes, I do. But he claimed it wasn't his. We have no way to prove it was, it was a cash receipt." Suzie pursed her lips and ran her hand back through her hair as she contemplated. "Maybe Carlene would remember him, though. What do you think? If she could remember him being there buying the oil, that would place him in the garage, and he wouldn't be able to deny being there."

"It's a good way to catch him in a lie, if it is a lie." Mary nodded. "I say we get together with Carlene tomorrow and find out whether she can recognize him."

"Okay, but tonight, we eat." Suzie patted her stomach. "I can't wait to enjoy this delicious meal." As she carried in the salad, the final guest arrived, and the group gathered around the table. Within minutes, all talk of homicide was forgotten as they swapped stories about the town, the beach, and Paul's fishing trips.

As the evening wound down, Mary found herself watching the front door. After Jason's comments about James, and Wes' general recoil around him, anxiety bubbled up within her. Could James have been connected in some way to Graham's murder? The idea seemed impossible. He'd shown up the day before Graham was killed. What could bring him from out of town just to kill Graham? She cleared the dinner dishes with Suzie's help, then brought out two freshly baked pies to share with everyone. After Anna had her slice, she went to her room to gather her things. Mary and Suzie walked her out to the porch as she prepared to leave.

"Thanks again for staying with us." Suzie smiled. "We hope you think of Dune House the next time you're in town."

"Oh, I plan to. It's such a nice relaxed environment. Plus, there's no way to beat this beach." Anna gazed out over the water for a moment, then looked back at them. "Thank you, both." She smiled, then waved as she headed down the steps to the parking lot.

"I sure hope we made a good impression." Mary

crossed her arms as she watched the young woman reach her car.

"She said we did." Suzie shrugged and slipped her hands into her pockets. "She seemed happy."

"I know, but I've been so distracted with all of this, I barely spoke to her. Usually, I make more of an effort."

"Don't be so hard on yourself, Mary, you did a great job." Suzie guided her back inside. "I think what you need is another slice of pie."

"Maybe you're right." Mary grinned.

Kyle and Jess headed up to their room, and Summer and Jason said goodnight. Suzie and Paul wandered off for a walk, and Mary found herself alone with her piece of pie. She added an extra dollop of whipped cream and wondered what Wes might be up to. When the front door swung open she almost expected it to be him. Instead, it was James.

"Evening." James nodded to her as he headed straight for the stairs.

"Oh James, there's pie!" She stood up quickly. "One's apple and the other is blueberry. You can have some of both if you'd like."

"No thanks." James paused at the bottom of the steps, then looked back at her. "Are you alone?"

"Jess and Kyle are upstairs." Mary felt her muscles tense as she considered the question a bit strange.

"Okay." He stood there a moment longer, his eyes locked to hers. "Have a good night." He turned and climbed up the stairs.

Mary watched him go, her heart in her throat, as her mind spun with uncertainty. Was that his attempt at being friendly? Or did he have another agenda?

~

"It's a beautiful night." Suzie savored the sensation of Paul's hand wrapped around hers. As Pilot ran ahead of them along the beach, she laughed at the spray of sand he kicked up with his large paws. She didn't think he would ever grow into them.

"Yes, it is." Paul leaned a little closer to her and smiled. "Then again, as long as I'm with you, it's always beautiful."

"Aw." Suzie laughed and rolled her eyes. "That's a little cheesy you know."

"Cheesy? Me?" He gasped, then laughed as well. "All right, maybe a little. I missed you."

"I missed you, too." She glanced over at him. "Sometimes the long trips can be hard."

"I can cut back if you think —"

"No." She met his eyes and smiled. "Paul, I know they're important to your business. Honestly, it just surprises me. I never thought I would miss anyone. It's kind of a luxury to be able to."

"A luxury?" Paul kissed her cheek. "I love the way you think."

"Good, I'll remember that." She winked at him. "Hey, you've been around here a long time, do you know about the race car scene in Parish?"

"Sure. A bit, I guess." He shrugged. "It's all amateur stuff."

"Do you know a Brennan Coopers?" She paused beside the water.

"Brennan, yes, I've heard that name bantered around. He's pretty good from what I know. He's been in the game for a while."

"Any rumors about his temper or anything like that? Did he ever have issues with anyone?" Suzie called Pilot back with a quick clap of her hands as he began to splash through the water.

"Some of those guys can be hot heads, especially when it comes to their cars. You're better off asking Wes about that, though."

"Good idea." Suzie nodded. "I will, the next time I see him."

"Can we talk about this?" He drew her closer to him and met her eyes.

"About what?" Suzie smiled as she searched his gaze.

"About you and Mary launching your own investigation?" Paul laced his fingers through hers. "I saw the two of you talking, I see that look in your eyes, I know what you're up to."

"Then what's to talk about? We are just going to look into things a bit." Suzie raised an eyebrow, then caressed his cheek. "There's no harm in that."

"Listen, whoever did this is vicious. Is that really the kind of person you want to be looking into?" Paul shook his head. "It's a big risk to take."

"So is going out there." Suzie tipped her head towards the wide-open ocean, which shimmered in the moonlight. "You never know what the weather might do, what other danger might come up. But you still step on that boat, don't you?"

"Yes." He sighed and turned to face the water. "But that's not the same thing."

"Sure, it is." She rubbed her hands along his shoulders as she stepped up behind him. "I'll never ask you not to go, Paul, because it's a part of you.

It's a risk, but it's what you love, and I could never take that from you. Maybe I run a bed and breakfast now, but once I was an investigative journalist, and that desire to find the truth, it still pumps through my veins."

"I see." Paul turned back to face her and slid his arms around her waist. "I understand what you're saying. But that doesn't make me like it."

"You don't have to like it." Suzie placed a light peck on his lips. "You just have to trust me to know my limitations, and to make good choices. I've made pretty good ones up to this point, haven't I?" She grinned. "They got me here, with you."

"The best choices." Paul sighed and stared into her eyes.

"I'll be fine, Paul, I promise."

"I know you will be. But if you run into anything strange, you just have to let me know. All right? I'm here if you need any help with anything."

"Thanks." Suzie closed her eyes as he hugged her.

Pilot let out a loud bark, then plowed between them.

"Uh oh, someone's jealous." Paul laughed and crouched down to pet the dog. "Don't worry, Pilot, I love you, too."

"Oh great, now I'm jealous." Suzie laughed. "Pilot, no love for me?"

"Don't be greedy, you get to see him all the time." Paul laughed as he straightened up.

As they walked back towards Dune House, Suzie's thoughts returned to Graham. If Brennan was the hot head that Paul described, then maybe he really did go after Graham over his car. Not only did he damage his vehicle, but his reputation among his peers took a hit because of the wreck. That might have been enough to push him over the edge. Maybe a little more research on him would reveal more about him. She guided Paul inside. When she opened the door to the house she spotted Mary near the kitchen. The expression on her face made her heart skip a beat.

"Mary, are you okay?"

"Yes, I'm fine." Mary laughed. "Sorry, just got a little spooked."

"I should get home." Paul leaned in close to Suzie for a kiss, then pulled back and looked at Mary. "Are you sure you're okay?"

"Yes, I'll be fine. Goodnight, Paul."

"Goodnight, ladies." He caught Suzie's eyes one more time, then headed for the door.

Once they were alone, Suzie looked straight at Mary.

"What really happened?"

"It was James. He came in, and it just spooked me. He asked me if I was alone. Isn't that a strange question?"

"That is strange. Did he ask you anything else?" Suzie studied her friend.

"It just seemed like he was feeling me out. I don't know. It just felt strange." Mary frowned. "It might have been my imagination."

"I doubt it was. You have great instincts, Mary." Suzie gave her a hug. "Let's call it a night. First thing in the morning we'll go see Carlene again and find out what we can about James. If he bought the oil there, she might know something."

"Okay, that's a good plan." Mary glanced at the stairs that James had just recently climbed.

"We'll be on our toes." Suzie looked up the stairs as well. "All of this has us pretty shaken up. But remember, the background check came back clean. Even if it is somehow fake, he has no reason to suspect that we know anything about him. Let's just play it cool until we can find out more."

"Play it cool," Mary repeated, then shivered.

CHAPTER 9

*E*arly the next morning, Suzie woke to the smell of coffee in the air. She dressed and headed downstairs. Mary poured her a mug of coffee as she descended the last step.

"Morning." She offered her the mug.

"Mary, did you sleep?" Suzie took the coffee. "Thank you."

"Not much." Mary grimaced. "I did try, though. I just find it hard to rest when I have so much going on in my head." She gestured to the breakfast platter of food she'd prepared for the guests. "It's pretty much self-serve so they should be fine. I don't think James has eaten a thing I've put out since he got here, so I'm not too concerned about him."

"This is great. But we can't go to Carlene's too

early. She might not even be awake." Suzie leaned against the counter and took a sip of her coffee.

"No, but we can take a drive by the garage and see if it's still roped off. I was thinking maybe if I see it again, I'll notice something I didn't before. Up for a drive?" Mary held up the keys.

"Yes, sure, that's a great idea." Suzie grabbed one of the blueberry muffins from the tray of food. "Something for the road."

"Now, that's a great idea." Mary grinned as she snatched up one for herself.

When they arrived at the garage the police tape had been taken down, but the garage doors were closed, and the office door was locked.

Mary took a deep breath of the morning air as she looked around the exterior of the small, square building. With the time of death confirmed, it was possible that the killer had still been on the property when she arrived. She might have caught something out of the corner of her eye. Something she just didn't think was important at the time.

"Were there other cars in the parking lot?" Suzie walked beside her.

"A few. But I can't remember how many. I think just one or two."

"Well, one would be Carlene's, and one Graham's." Suzie nodded.

"Oh, and there were more." Mary turned to the side of the parking lot and saw a line of cars. "There. I think they're all still there."

"There's the SUV. They must be vehicles that Graham was working on."

"I'm not sure that we can ever take that home." Mary gritted her teeth.

"Don't worry about that, now. Just try to focus. Is there anything different now than there was the day that Graham died? Take one more look around." Suzie placed her hand on her friend's shoulder. "I'm right here with you."

"It all looks the same." Mary sighed as she surveyed her surroundings. "Honestly, if there was anything different, I don't think I'd know it. I just keep seeing Carlene on the concrete floor. I knew Graham was gone, and I thought Carlene was, too, until I checked on her. I was so relieved that she was still alive. Whoever did this to Graham was obviously only after him."

"Or they didn't have time to finish the job." Suzie met her eyes. "Carlene is very lucky that you showed up when you did."

"If only Graham had been so lucky." Mary

frowned as she headed back to the car. "After we check on Carlene, let's see what we can find out about James. If he had anything to do with this, I don't want him under the same roof with us."

"You're right about that." Suzie drove towards Carlene's house. It was only a few minutes from the garage. When she parked, Mary stepped out of the car. Suzie stepped out as well and took a look around the house. After visiting the garage, she had a renewed desire to be cautious.

She squinted as sunlight bounced off the windshield of a nearby taxi and struck her in the eyes.

"What a bright morning." Suzie shielded her eyes then headed in the direction of Carlene's house.

"It's supposed to be ninety by this afternoon. I'm not sure I'm ready for this heat." Mary waved her hand in front of her face as she followed Suzie up the driveway to the front door.

Once more Suzie noticed the decor of the house and smiled.

"I wonder if she's home," Mary said.

"There's a car in the driveway. It's the same one that was here yesterday, so I'd guess she is." Suzie raised her hand to knock on the door, but hesitated when she saw that the door was partially open. A voice inside made her tense up. She put a finger to her lips as she glanced at Mary.

Mary nodded, and crept closer to the door.

"Who did it, Carlene?"

"I don't know."

"Don't lie to me. I know that you're holding something back." His tone grew sharper.

"James?" Suzie mouthed the name to Mary.

"I think so," Mary whispered back. Her heart began to pound. She had no idea what James was doing there, but she suspected that it wasn't something good. Every second that passed led to greater risk for Carlene. She knew that she couldn't just stand there and hope that nothing bad happened to the woman. Instead of even taking the time to call the police, she pushed the door open and stepped inside.

"Carlene! Are you home? Carlene!"

"Mary!" Suzie gasped, then followed after her. She caught up with her in the living room, where James spun around to face them. Her chest tightened with fear when she saw the gun that he held in his hand.

"Drop it!" Mary shouted and reached for her purse as if she might have a weapon inside.

"Hold it, just hold on!" James held one hand up

in the air as he lowered his weapon. "There's no need for any of that." He looked at Mary and when she didn't pull out a weapon from her purse, his shoulders relaxed slightly. "I'm just going to put it away." He slowly put the gun back in its holster. Suzie and Mary watched him until the gun was safely secured.

"Carlene, are you okay?" Mary looked over at her.

"Yes, I'm fine." She stepped around James, and over to the two women. "This guy just showed up at my door and started interrogating me. Threatening me."

"Stay back behind me." Suzie moved in front of her, her eyes fixated on the gun in his holster. "James, what exactly is going on here?"

"He can tell it to Wes." Mary frowned as she pulled out her cell phone. "I'm calling him, now." She tried to hide the tremble in her voice by clearing her throat, but even that sounded shaky.

"Good idea." Suzie nodded. "Tell him about the gun."

"I'm licensed to carry that weapon, it's legal. Go ahead and call the police, I haven't done anything wrong here. Have I, Carlene?" James locked eyes with her.

"No." Carlene sniffled as she held up her hands. "Suzie, Mary, it's okay. He wasn't doing anything to harm me."

"Then why do you have a gun?" Suzie took a step closer to James.

"It is registered. It is legal." He looked between the two of them. "You're both mixed up in something you have no idea about here. Maybe if we could all calm down, I could explain it to you."

"I heard the way you were talking to Carlene." Mary narrowed her eyes as she stared at him. "There was nothing polite about it. Now, you can tell us the truth, or you can tell it to Wes, but either way you're going to explain yourself."

"I intend to." He frowned. "I'm not who you think I am."

"Then, who are you?" Suzie crossed her arms.

Mary glanced nervously at Suzie, then looked back at James as he began to speak.

"I am a private investigator. I'm just going to take out my wallet." James moved his hand slowly to his pocket on the opposite side to his holster, then pulled out a flat, black, leather wallet. "Here, take a look." He offered it to Suzie.

"A private investigator?" She took the wallet from him and with a flick of her wrist flipped it open. "How does that explain anything? You still have no right to point a weapon at her."

"I was hired by someone to investigate Graham's involvement in a spate of car thefts that included some of the cars he repaired." He looked back towards Carlene. "He has some very angry and influential customers."

Suzie looked through the cards in his wallet and found one that declared he was a private investigator.

"Marlin Casen?" Suzie met his eyes as he looked back at her. "Is that your real name?"

"Yes, it is." He looked between her and Mary. "Like I said, this is nothing personal, it's business."

"It's personal when you threaten someone with a weapon." Mary continued to shield Carlene. "After all she has been through, how could you put her through more?"

"Carlene isn't as innocent as you may think. She's protecting someone." Marlin cast a brief smirk in her direction. "The point is, I followed the evidence right to Graham's Garage. I went there to speak to him, and to get a feel of the place, the day before he died. But I never had the chance to speak to him. Someone prevented that from happening." He looked back at Carlene.

"And I believe she knows exactly who that someone is."

"You weren't there the morning it happened. Carlene was knocked out cold." Mary narrowed her eyes. "Why would she protect someone who hurt her like that? I think you're grasping at straws because you came to a dead end, and you know that your employer is not going to like that."

"Really?" Marlin cleared his throat, then looked past Mary, to Carlene. "Why don't you tell the truth, Carlene? Why don't you tell us who you are protecting?"

"I don't have anything to say to you." Carlene took a deep breath. "I want you to leave my house."

"I'll leave." Marlin shifted his weight from one foot to the other as he gazed at her. "I can leave right now, with everything I know, and come back with an officer to put you in handcuffs." He raised his eyebrows. "Is that what you want?"

"No." Her voice shuddered. "Please, just leave me alone. I don't know anything about what happened. I don't know why you think I do."

"Keep saying that, you might eventually believe it." Marlin narrowed his eyes. "I'll leave. But this isn't over, Carlene. If you don't want the truth to come out, then you need to contact me with the information I need. There's no reason that you have to get hurt in all of this, I can and will protect you, but you have to do your part."

"Protect her from what?" Suzie's tone sharpened as she stepped in front of Marlin. "Are you threatening her again?"

"I'm not the one she has to worry about." Marlin's eyes cut in Suzie's direction, his cheeks flushed. "The person who killed Graham, is who she needs to be worried about. Because whoever that is, is going to see her as a risk. He's going to come after you, Carlene. Don't let him lie to you, he's going to do whatever it takes to protect himself." He turned back to face her, his jaw clenched as he stared at her. "Stop protecting him!"

"Enough!" Mary wrapped her arm around Carlene's shoulders. She felt a shudder course through the younger woman. "Get out of here, now!"

"I'm calling the police right now." Suzie pulled out her phone and began to dial.

"No please! Don't!" Carlene gasped as fresh tears spilled down her cheeks. "Please, Suzie!"

"Okay." Suzie nodded.

"I'll make sure that the gun is legally yours."

Mary looked at Marlin. "If it isn't I will make sure the police know about it."

"Fine." Marlin smirked, then took a deep breath. He locked his eyes to hers. "You two may think you have this all figured out, but Carlene cannot be trusted. She's protecting someone."

"Says the man who held her at gunpoint." Suzie sneered. "Sorry, but your word doesn't have a lot of standing here."

"We really should call the police," Mary said. "I don't know what's happened here between the two of you, but it's not for your sake that we're not. It's Carlene's home, and if she doesn't want us to call, then we won't. But you need to be prepared to leave Dune House this evening."

"Whatever you say." Marlin held his hands up in the air as he backed towards the door. "Carlene, don't forget what I said." He looked straight at the woman as he reached the door. "I'm not your enemy here. I just might be the only one that can help you."

"Just go!" Carlene covered her face as her shoulders began to shake.

"You heard her." Suzie eyed him as he lingered near the door.

"Ladies." Marlin nodded to Suzie, then to Mary. "You'll see that the gun is legally mine and that you are scared of the wrong person." He turned and pulled the door closed behind him as he left.

Mary breathed a sigh of relief. "Is he gone, Suzie?"

"It looks like it." Suzie peered through the front window. "No sign of him out there."

"Carlene, why didn't you let us call the police?" Mary took a step towards her, but the woman shied back the moment she did.

"I don't want to talk about it, okay? I just want to move on from Graham's murder. I don't want the police involved. If you get the police involved, it will just make everything worse for me." Carlene pursed her lips. "Please go. I need to be alone."

"Carlene, if you're in some kind of trouble, we can help you." Suzie softened the edges of her words, hoping that the woman would be willing to confide in her. "We want you to be safe."

"I am safe. If everyone would just leave me alone, I would be perfectly safe." Carlene crossed her arms as her eyebrows knitted together. "Can you go, please?"

"Carlene—" Mary began.

"Mary, let's go. Let's allow her to have some rest." Suzie turned towards the door. "She needs some time to calm down."

"Okay, yes." Mary gazed at Carlene a moment longer, then followed Suzie out the door. As she walked to the car she considered calling Wes, but decided against it. She didn't quite know what to make of what had just unfolded, and wanted some time to think about it.

In silence the two women settled in the car. As Suzie slid the key into the ignition, she glanced over at Mary.

"What was that about? Do you think someone is threatening Carlene if she goes to the police? Maybe the murderer?"

"I don't know. But something is going on." Mary frowned as she glanced up and down the street. "Maybe I should just call Wes." She dug her phone from her purse. "He'll check into Marlin and know if the gun is legal or not and if he needs to be arrested."

"But Carlene didn't want the cops involved." Suzie looked back at Carlene's small house and caught sight of the flutter of a curtain. "Which means she definitely has something to hide."

"You're right, and I think we're in over our heads here. I mean Marlin had Carlene at gunpoint. I need Wes to check the ownership of the gun."

"I could ask Jason to do it." Suzie drove back

towards Garber. "But if you think it's best to call Wes, go ahead."

"I just think he needs to know." Mary cringed as she realized that the time to call him was back in Carlene's house. Instead of making the call, she sent him a text, which asked him to meet her at Dune House.

CHAPTER 10

Mary paced slowly back and forth through the dining room. She knew that Wes would be there any minute, and she had yet to decide how she would explain the circumstances of her knowing that Marlin has a gun and that his real name is not James. She'd asked him to run Marlin's name to see if he legally owned a weapon, but she hadn't revealed what had transpired at Carlene's house. A loud knock on the door made her jump. She took a sharp breath, and Pilot jumped up from his bed. He trotted towards the door with his tail wagging. He was used to guests arriving, and recognized Wes' knock, so he eagerly went to greet him instead of barking.

Wes opened the door, and Mary stepped

towards him as he made his way inside. He pulled off his hat, tucked it under his arm, then looked into her eyes.

"Tell me everything, Mary."

"Did you find out anything?" She led him through the front entrance to the dining room. "About Marlin?"

"First, you need to tell me what this is about." He frowned as he patted Pilot's head. "Why are you being so evasive? Are you okay?"

"I'm fine, but there is a problem. I need to find out about a gun."

"You want to buy a gun?"

"No, I don't want to buy it. What would I want with a gun?" Mary scrunched up her nose and shook her head. "Marlin has a gun. Well, James does, but James isn't actually James. But he still has a gun."

"Wait a minute." Wes held up his hands. "I think you need to start at the beginning and tell me exactly what happened here."

As Mary filled Wes in on the event at Carlene's house, she noticed his eyes narrowing more and more with each word she spoke. By the time she finished, they were full of anger.

"Why exactly didn't you call the police? Or

me?" Wes placed his hands on her shoulders, and though his touch was gentle, his tone was firm. "Do you have any idea how much danger you were in?"

"I was there, Wes, remember?" Mary frowned as she curved her hands around his and gave them a gentle squeeze. "We didn't expect any of that to happen. But once we were there, we had to do our best to diffuse it. Which we did. Now of course, I know about the gun, and I don't know if he is allowed to have it, and I'm worried about him using it. As long as it checks out, he can keep it. Right?"

"Yes." Wes sighed as he drew his hands from hers. "I can't believe that Carlene didn't want the police called. That certainly is odd." He crossed his arms as he looked into her eyes. "But it shouldn't have mattered what she wanted. You should have called me. I would have been there to help you."

"We were able to handle it, Wes." She smiled some. "I have more tricks up my sleeve than you may think."

"I'm sure you do." He sighed as he looked up towards the ceiling. "But it isn't just about that. You knew that Carlene is a part of an active investigation, my investigation. Honestly, not calling me, or the police, borders on obstruction of justice. I just don't understand what you were thinking."

"Obstruction of justice?" She raised an eyebrow, then took a step back from him.

"Yes." He caught her hand and tugged her gently back towards him. "I can't say I'm not bothered by this. She's obviously hiding something, and the moment that I get my hands on James or Marlin, or whoever he is, he's going to pay for having a weapon anywhere near you."

"My weapon, don't you mean?" A voice from the front door drew both of their attention. Marlin Casen filled the door frame, but didn't take a step further inside.

"Put your hands up!" Wes drew his gun so fast that Mary stumbled back in reaction.

"Easy, cowboy." Marlin raised his hands slowly in the air. "You've got no reason to point that gun at me. I'm not threatening you, and I'm not here to cause any trouble. I have a right to my gun. Your damsel here, should stop sticking her nose in other people's business."

"Keep quiet." Wes narrowed his eyes.

"Wes, calm down." Mary placed her hand gently on his shoulder. "He's right. Unless Carlene is willing to press charges against him, there's nothing that can be done. There's no need to get yourself into trouble for my sake, remember it was my choice to walk into that house."

"I'll speak to Carlene, I'll get her to press charges." Wes kept the gun pointed steadily at Marlin. "Put your hands on your head and turn around."

"Detective, I can help you with your case. We don't need to be enemies here." He kept his hands in the air, but did not turn, instead he looked straight at Wes. "Be smart about this. Do you want to solve a murder or show off for your girlfriend?"

"You have quite the mouth on you, don't you?" Wes lowered the gun some. "What do you know about the case?"

"Ah, you're one of the true detectives left, huh? Willing to be reasonable?" Marlin lowered his hands some as well. "I shouldn't really share information like this. You're going to have to calm down, if you want to hear what I have to say."

"Listen to him, Wes, he knows something about Carlene. He thinks she knows who killed Graham." Mary kept her hand on Wes' shoulder, as she could feel how tense his muscles were beneath his shirt. She trusted Wes, but she had no idea how he would react if someone threatened her. Would he be willing to pull the trigger? The thought made her heart pound.

"I'll listen." Wes slowly lowered his weapon, then holstered it. "So, let's hear it."

"May I come in?" Marlin shifted his attention to Mary.

"Yes." Mary lingered close to Wes. As much as she wanted to know what Marlin had to say about Carlene, she also didn't trust him. He seemed to have an answer for everything, while giving no actual information.

"Thank you." Marlin lowered his hands to his sides then stepped further into the house. Pilot growled as he sniffed around Marlin's feet.

"Pilot, come here boy." Suzie summoned the dog as she stepped into the dining room. "Marlin?" She looked from him, to Mary and Wes. "Is everything okay here?"

"Yes, Marlin's about to tell us exactly how Carlene was involved in Graham's murder." Mary stared at him. "Isn't that right?"

"No, I'm afraid that's wrong." Marlin watched the dog as he eased his way further into the room. "But you're still going to want to hear what I have to say."

"We're listening." Wes positioned himself

between the two women and Marlin. "Maybe you could start with an explanation for the fake name and fake identification?"

"That's just part of the job. I thought Suzie and Mary might look me up, and that they might try to avoid giving me a room if they discovered I was a private investigator. I also thought that they might know or be connected to Graham. I wanted to see if I could get information from them. When I'm on a job, I don't rent rooms under my name, just in case anything goes sideways with the person that I'm investigating. It's for my safety, as well as those that run or work at the place I stay at." Marlin leaned back against the dining room table. "I'm sure that you can understand that, Wes. If you're undercover, do you use your name?"

"No. But you're not a police officer." He continued to study him.

"I came here to investigate a car theft ring." Marlin shrugged as a faint smile played across his lips. "I suppose if I was a police officer that might be my job, huh?"

"Jason mentioned that." Suzie narrowed her eyes. "There's been quite a bit of trouble around here involving car thefts."

"Yes, and in Parish, too." Wes frowned. "Are you saying all of these thefts are connected?"

"That would be my theory." Marlin tilted his head from side to side. "But then again, I'm not a police officer. I followed some evidence to Graham's Garage. Several of the people who had cars stolen were currently customers, or had been in the past, of his garage. It seemed too big of a number to be a coincidence."

"Yes, I noticed that, too. But if you were a local you wouldn't find it so strange. Graham's is the most highly recommended garage in Parish, and many people in Garber as well as other neighboring towns use it." Wes shook his head. "It's easy to see a clue where there isn't one. With such a wide assortment of customers, he was bound to have a few who had their vehicles stolen."

"Maybe." Marlin straightened up. "But the number was still too high for me. I came here to discuss the situation with him, but he was killed before I had the chance to do that."

"And Carlene was hurt as well." Mary spoke up, her voice stronger than she expected. "Let's not forget that."

"Right." Marlin rubbed his hand along the back of his neck. "When I stopped in there the day before, I bought the oil and tried to scope the place out, I spoke to Carlene. I noticed that she had a tattoo on the underside of her wrist. Did any of you notice that?"

"No." Suzie frowned. "I don't remember seeing it."

"Me either." Mary's eyes widened.

"It was documented." Wes nodded. "It's a circle of thorns and roses. She said it was a tattoo she shared with a friend of hers."

"A few friends, maybe." Marlin eyed Wes for a moment. "It's a gang tattoo. It's the symbol of South Cannon's Boys. I'm not surprised you didn't recognize it, they're from a few cities over, and they're not a well-known gang."

"But you know of them?" Suzie stepped forward. "Why is that?"

"I've dealt with them before on another matter. They target the wealthy. They don't stick to a particular neighborhood. They roam, and target vulnerable, high income communities. They steal anything they can get their hands on and are often violent in the process."

"Well, that certainly isn't Parish." Wes narrowed his eyes.

"Or Garber." Suzie raised an eyebrow. "Isn't it

possible that she just has a similar tattoo? Just because it's a gang symbol, doesn't mean that she knew that when she got it."

"No, I don't think it's possible. The colors, the placement, they are the same. Mark my words, she's involved in the gang, and she's protecting whoever killed Graham. Parish and Garber might not be wealthy communities, but there are a few well-off customers that use Graham's Garage. If I'm right, and this gang has something to do with the car thefts in the area, then they likely targeted Graham." He held up his hands. "I don't have the evidence to get Carlene arrested for anything, and honestly that's not why I'm here. I'm here because I need to recover a few vehicles for my employer. I've been trying to track down Brody, to find out what he knows. But I haven't been able to get hold of him. I believe he might be the one that Carlene is protecting, because she is scared of him or she cares about him. Once I have that information and get the cars back my job will be done. What happens to Carlene, is not really my concern."

"Nice." Mary frowned. "I suppose that's why you didn't hesitate to point your gun at her?"

"I didn't hesitate to point my gun at her because she's involved with a criminal gang that is known to be violent, ruthlessly violent. I'm not stupid enough to believe that she wouldn't come after me if she had the chance."

"You have an interesting theory, Marlin, but it falls apart when you take into account Brody's alibi. Carlene claimed he was at a class all day, and I confirmed with the teacher of that class that he was there." Wes frowned, then shook his head. "I haven't caught up with him yet, but I think you've got yourself pointed in the wrong direction."

"Alibis can be faked, with the influence of this gang, it's definitely possible. Now, you know what I know. You need to be cautious of these people." He glanced back at Wes. "I am allowed to own the gun."

"I confirmed you legally own a gun. But if I ever hear of you wielding that gun, or any other weapon, anywhere near either of these two women, I will make sure that you never know freedom again. Do you understand me?" His eyes locked to Marlin's.

"I understand." Marlin stared back, his voice even as he continued. "To be fair, they were the ones that walked in on the situation. Perhaps you, a seasoned detective, should warn them about involving themselves in things they have no business being involved in."

"You might be right about that." Wes shot a brief look in Mary's direction. "Now, who is your employer?" He looked back at Marlin.

"Sorry, that's confidential." Marlin shook his head.

"I need to know his name to verify your reason for being here." Wes took a step towards him. "You can tell me here, or down at the station."

"I'll tell you what, Detective." Marlin tipped his chin upward with pride as he studied Wes. "When you have enough evidence to put some handcuffs on me, then we'll talk about it."

"Shouldn't take long." Wes narrowed his eyes.

"We'll see about that, Detective."

"You can't stay here, anymore." Wes pointed up the stairs. "I'll take you up to get your stuff."

"Okay." Marlin nodded as he followed Wes up the stairs and Suzie and Mary stood together listening for any sign of an argument or scuffle between them.

Marlin came down a few minutes later with Wes close behind him.

"Suzie, Mary." Marlin nodded to each of them as he walked towards the door. "Thanks for your hospitality. You run a nice place."

He didn't turn back before stepping outside and

closing the door behind him. In the silence that followed, Wes drummed his fingertips on the dining room table.

"He's not wrong, you know?"

"I should take Pilot out for a walk." Suzie started towards the dog.

"Wait just a minute, Suzie." Wes called out to her, while keeping his eyes on Mary. "This isn't just about Mary. You were there, too."

"Yes, I was." Suzie turned back to face him. "And?"

"And, you both know this is my investigation." Wes looked between them. "Didn't that even cross your minds." He growled as his cell phone buzzed. Once he checked it, he looked back at them. "This discussion isn't over, I mean it. You two need to be more careful. I have to go." He brushed a light kiss along Mary's cheek, then hurried out to the parking lot.

"Have a good day, Wes." Mary watched as he disappeared, then turned to face Suzie. "Well, that was uncomfortable."

"What a crazy day." Suzie pressed her palm against her forehead and let out a long, slow breath. "I don't think I've had such an adventure in a long time."

"Adventure, that's one way to put it." Mary smiled. "I'm not sure that I'll be able to sleep tonight."

"It was scary, wasn't it?" Suzie frowned as she lowered her hand. "It's funny, there was a time when I was in dangerous situations pretty often, but I guess I'm getting older."

"Oh please, you'll never get older." Mary laughed as she rolled her eyes, then walked into the kitchen to prepare them both some tea. "I think it was just unexpected. I mean, we did let Marlin stay under our roof, with no idea that he had a gun, no idea that he wasn't who he claimed to be, that's scary enough. Then to see him threatening Carlene like that, it was upsetting."

"Yes, it was. But now that we know what we know, I can't help but wonder if Brody was involved somehow." Suzie raised an eyebrow then smiled as she accepted a cup of tea. "Maybe Marlin really was on to something."

"Even if he was on to something, he had no right to draw his gun on Carlene. If it weren't for her refusing to press charges he would be in jail right now. As for Brody, maybe he did come up with a way to fake his alibi, maybe Carlene had no idea that it was a lie. She didn't see the person who hit her. Unfortunately, as long as Brody's alibi holds up, he'll never be considered a suspect. Marlin claims to be a private investigator, but that doesn't mean he can be trusted. Wes did the right thing by asking him to leave." Mary frowned, then set her cup down as she sat forward. "I think we need to be more careful. It was unnerving to go through that today. I know you and I can handle just about anything, but Wes has a point about us both being more cautious."

"Are you saying you want to step back and not look into Graham's murder?" Suzie looked over at her with surprise. She knew that Mary wanted this murder solved.

"Not at all." Mary met her friend's eyes with intense determination. "I just think we need to be smarter about it. We didn't know what we were getting into when we tried to find out more information from Carlene. So, we need to promise each other that neither of us will go into any situation without taking a breath and checking with the other. How does that sound?"

"That sounds more like you." Suzie smiled and nodded. "You're right. I promise." She squeezed Mary's hand. "Finding the truth is very important, but keeping each other safe should be our first priority."

"Yes, it should. Do you think Carlene really was involved?" Mary finished her tea.

"I think that we definitely need to find out more. Marlin could just be trying to throw us off his scent." Suzie finished her tea as well. "I don't trust that man one bit."

"Me either. I think we need to start again in the morning. We both need a break after this crazy day. Let's take Pilot for a walk and then have a nice meal and get some rest." Mary stretched her arms above her head.

"Good idea." Suzie nodded.

"Come on, Pilot." Pilot wagged his tail as he followed after them.

After dinner Suzie and Mary were tired and decided to have an early night. They had spoken about everything except for the events of the afternoon and the murder, but it was on both their minds.

Within minutes of sprawling out on her bed Suzie fell into a fitful sleep.

CHAPTER 11

*H*ours later, a sharp jolt of her muscles woke Suzie. Clearly, the recent events were playing on her mind. She pressed her hand against her chest until she felt her heartbeat settle. She pulled herself out of bed, got dressed and headed for the kitchen. She found Mary already at the coffee pot.

"Wow, I thought for once that I was up earlier than you." Suzie laughed some as she stepped up beside her friend. "I guess I was wrong."

"I had a hard time sleeping." Mary nodded as she turned to face her. "It looks like you did, too. Are you okay, Suzie?" She frowned.

"I am." Suzie shook her head. "I had a horrible sleep. I think all of this is just getting to me." She pushed her hair back behind her ears. "So, I'm going to dig into Graham a bit more. I know that we've already looked into him, but I feel like we're missing something. We know he had plenty of satisfied customers, and a few who weren't so happy, but what about his own extended family?"

"Carlene said he didn't have any." Mary poured them both a mug of coffee. "We're going to need this today."

"Yes, we are." Suzie smiled and leaned back against the counter. "Yes, Carlene said he had no family, but that can't really be true, can it? Everyone has some kind of family. I had Jason and didn't even realize it. Maybe someone from his past came back to pay him a visit and things went sour? We can't exactly trust what Carlene has to say, can we? I mean she might not know about his family?"

"No, you're right. We can't." Mary carried her coffee into the dining room. "Kyle and Jess aren't joining us for breakfast, so we have some free time."

"Okay." Suzie retrieved her computer, then set it up on the table. "We didn't dig far enough, I don't think. We went on the assumption that there would be no one from Graham's background that would have a motive."

"How are we going to dig, though? We don't have much to go on."

"Well, we know he's always lived in Parish. There's only one high school in Parish. So, we should be able to find some information there." Suzie began to type. A few minutes later she sighed and sat back in her chair. "Well, it looks like he didn't graduate, there were no other family members in the school, and I can't find any information on any family."

"He really didn't have a family." Mary stared down into the remains of her coffee. "He lived his whole life with no one to call family besides his wife."

"Even worse, it looks like Brennan hasn't held back on his rantings, even though Graham is dead. He's still posting some terrible things about him, even accusing him of attempting to kill him." She drew back from the screen and scrunched up her nose. "How distasteful for him to behave that way."

"He's angry." Mary peered at the screen. "Angry enough to cause some great harm, I'm sure. We don't know for sure that this had anything to do with a car theft ring. I haven't seen any evidence that Graham was involved in anything like that."

"No, me either." Suzie tapped her fingertips on

the side of the computer. "I think we've reached our limit for what we can find out now. We should take a break."

"I hope this is put to rest soon." Mary looked out towards the water. "I'm ready for things to get peaceful around here, again."

"Yes, me too. I'm going to take Pilot for a walk." Suzie called Pilot to her side. As they started off across the beach she felt some of the tension ease from her muscles.

She gazed out over the calm water. The peace was soothing after the upheaval of the past few days. She was startled as her phone rang. She looked to see it was Jason.

"Hi Suzie."

"Hi Jason." She watched as Pilot took off after a seagull.

"Wes told me what happened with Marlin."

"He did?" Suzie quickened her pace to keep up with Pilot. "I'm surprised by that."

"I was surprised, too, that you hadn't told me about it. We both think that you and Mary put yourselves in a very dangerous—"

"All right, yes, I've heard this already." Suzie sighed. "Is that why you were calling? To lecture me?"

"No. I know better. You're going to do as you please. I'm calling you because as soon as Wes told me about Marlin, I started digging into him. It turns out he's a retired police officer."

"Retired? But he's so young." Suzie kept a close eye on Pilot, but stopped beside the water.

"Yes, well there aren't too many details about why, but I do know where he was employed and who his captain was, so I'm going to see if I can get some more information about him. Until then, I want you to be extra cautious. He has training, and a law enforcement background."

"I see. Thanks for telling me, Jason. I will be careful." Suzie patted her leg to call Pilot back to her. As soon as he reached her she bent down to pat him. "Did Wes tell you about Carlene?"

"Yes, he did. That's interesting information. I'm staying out of it though as it's Wes' investigation. I just wanted to look into Marlin since the first background check I did on James came back clean. Just remember to be careful."

"I will. Thanks, Jason." Suzie hung up the phone then led Pilot back towards Dune House. As she walked along her heartbeat quickened. What else was Marlin hiding from them? Knowing that he had training as a police officer meant he knew exactly how to use his gun. If he wanted to, he could come after any of them.

⁓

*W*hen Suzie returned to the house, she found Mary on the front porch with Wes.

"Hi there, Wes." She paused at the bottom of the steps and looked up at them.

"Hi Suzie. I guess you spoke to Jason?" Wes met her eyes.

"He just told me that Marlin used to be a police officer. Did you know that?" She ascended the steps.

"No, not until he told me. We have some new options for the investigation. I've ruled out any alibi for Brennan. I'm going to speak to him again as soon as I've gathered enough information." He reached down to pet Pilot.

"I'm going to head in and make some breakfast." Suzie winked briefly at Mary as she stepped past her. As she stepped inside her cell phone rang. She picked it up when she saw that it was Paul.

"Hi hon, what are you up to?"

"I'm checking on you. I haven't heard from you. What's going on?"

"Nothing much." Suzie shrugged.

"So, I heard about the gun situation." He cleared his throat.

"Heard about it? From who? Wes?"

"It should have been from you, don't you think?"

"Maybe." Suzie put some bread in the toaster and began to cook some eggs. "It's just been so crazy I haven't had a chance, and you've been busy, too."

"Never too busy for you. Are you sure you're okay? You sound a little tired."

"I didn't sleep much. But I'm fine." Suzie took a deep breath. "Can we have dinner, tomorrow?"

"How about tonight? If you're free?"

"Absolutely."

After Suzie finished her call with Paul she headed out onto the porch with breakfast for herself, Mary, and Wes.

"Some sustenance." Suzie smiled as she placed it down on the table. "You two will have to forgive me, I'm just going to grab a slice of toast. I need to take a shower to try to wake up a bit."

"Why don't you take a nap?" Mary smiled. "There's no need to rush off this morning."

"I'm not much for napping so early in the day, it

tends to make me more tired. But a nice shower will wake me right up. Enjoy your breakfast." Suzie snatched a piece of toast, then headed back into the house.

"Is Suzie holding up okay?" Wes sat down at the table as Mary sat across from him.

"Yes, I think so. She had some trouble sleeping last night."

"And you? Have you had any trouble after what you saw?"

"Not exactly. Mostly, I just want to know who did this to Graham." Mary looked into his eyes. "Any other news?"

"I spoke with Marlin's captain, and he confirmed that he is a retired police officer. He also vouched for him as a good police officer. I'm not sure how much I believe that because of what he did, but it certainly doesn't sound as if he has a history of being a loose cannon." He rubbed his hand along his forehead, then shook his head. "Mary, I feel like I'm hitting nothing but dead ends in this case. Graham's finances were an issue, but not enough of one for me to believe that he had any dealings with criminals or loan sharks." He stood up and walked to the edge of the deck. "I've thought about the fact that maybe Brody's alibi was fake. The class had over forty students in it, all in coveralls and working on cars. I think it's possible that he could have slipped out."

"Wes, take a breath." Mary stood up. "There's so much running through your mind right now. You're going to exhaust yourself."

"This is my job, Mary." He turned to face her. "I'm usually pretty good at it."

"I know you are. Sometimes I get so caught up in my own head, I can't remember my own name. I worry so much about what I'm not thinking about, that there's no room in my mind for anything else." Mary trailed her thumbs along his cheeks in a soothing stroke. "Just take a walk on the beach with me. I'm sure that it will help clear your head."

"But I should be checking leads and—"

"What leads?" Mary stared straight into his eyes. "Or do you mean going back over the same things you've already analyzed thousands of times? Unless you can find some way to place Brody at the garage that morning, there's nothing to chase."

"Mary." He sighed.

"Wes." She smiled. "It's a walk on the beach. It's not going to make you lose focus. I promise. I always think more clearly when I'm in motion. It helps me to relax and let the most important things come to the surface. It'll settle the noise in your head. I promise." She slipped her hand into his. "Just this once, maybe try taking my advice?"

"I take your advice all the time." Wes curled his hand around hers. "You're the one that decides to walk into a dangerous situation and then not call me."

"I'm sorry."

"I keep thinking about you walking into the garage so soon after the killer, and then to be at Carlene's house when Marlin had his gun drawn." His jaw clenched as he took a short breath. "And to be honest, the fact that you didn't call me. That is the part that gets to me the most. I've tried to let it go, I really have, Mary. But I just don't understand it. Don't you trust me?"

"I do." Mary searched his eyes, then swallowed hard. Was it possible that she didn't? Trust had been a hard thing for her after her marriage had been shattered by her husband's behavior. She didn't know how to look into a man's eyes and be certain that he would never hurt her. And yet, she wanted to feel that way with Wes. She had no reason not to. It wasn't fair to punish him for something he never did. "I didn't call you because Carlene was so frightened. I thought if I did, we would never get any information out of her. I wasn't thinking like your girlfriend, Wes, I was thinking like a detective."

"Yes, you were." He smiled as he studied her. "You missed your calling, you know?"

"Maybe." She laughed. "Perhaps I should have been working as a detective instead of raising my kids. Or maybe raising kids is the reason I think like a detective."

"That's very possible." Wes chuckled, then slid his arm through hers. "All right, a walk on the beach. I'm going to take your advice."

CHAPTER 12

After a shower, Suzie dressed and headed back out to the porch. Mary piled up the plates from breakfast and turned to carry them inside.

"Where's Wes?" Suzie smiled as she grabbed the remainder of the dishes.

"He had to go. We had a nice walk on the beach first, though." Mary set the dishes in the sink then took the rest from Suzie and added them to the sink. The subtle clang of the silverware against the stainless-steel sink jarred her nerves.

"I had a thought. I think we need to find out once and for all what Brennan is up to. If he is the killer, then he might do something to implicate himself. We've been so focused on Marlin and

Brody, but the only one that we know of with a real motive to kill Graham is Brennan. Of course, we can't be sure it's any of them, but I think Brennan is the easiest one to find more information about." Suzie grabbed a sponge and began to wipe down the counters as a rush of water from the faucet began to fill the sink.

"What are you suggesting?" Mary squirted some soap on a cloth and began to wash a plate.

"I think we should follow him. If he's so bold that he is willing to post his feelings about Graham even after he's been killed, then I'm willing to bet he's not going to be too cautious about hiding his guilt. We might be able to catch him in the act of trying to cover something up." Suzie grabbed a towel and began to dry the dishes that Mary washed.

"That's a good point. Wes did mention that his alibi couldn't be verified. We know that Brody has an alibi, and Carlene was knocked out, and honestly we have no idea where Marlin was at the time of the murder. But at least with Brennan we know that he had a problem with Graham, he was furious at him the day before, and that temper might be wild enough to make him commit murder." She handed over the final dish.

"I'm ready to find out what Brennan is up to." Suzie grinned.

"It's worth a shot to find out." Mary patted the top of Pilot's head, then smiled at him. "Can you guard the house while we're gone, boy?"

"Oh yes, quite the security dog." Suzie grinned as she stroked the dog's back. "He might just lick them to death."

"So true." Mary laughed, then stood up. "Let me gather up a few things for us to snack on in the car."

"I'll see if I can figure out where Brennan is by checking his social media." Suzie pulled out her phone and began to skim through all of the usual places for his name and picture. By the time Mary returned, Suzie knew what Brennan had been up to for the past few hours.

"Right now, he's having lunch at a place called the Parish Food Stop. I don't think I've ever been there before. Have you?" She looked up at Mary, then laughed at the large bag of snacks that she'd gathered.

"You never know what we might be in the mood for." Mary smiled as she set the bag on the table. "No, I've never heard of it, but I know there are a few little places in Parish that I haven't been to. Let's go, maybe we can catch him there if we hurry."

"All right, Pilot, we'll be back later." Suzie lead Pilot to the yard then went to their car. As she buckled her seat belt she realized that they were essentially stalking Brennan. Luckily, they could use the excuse of being obsessed fans if they were caught.

"I found the place." Mary held up her phone. "Head into Parish, and then we'll be going west. It's all the way at the edge of the city."

"Great." Suzie turned on the engine, then pulled out of the parking lot. "It'll be nice to see some parts of Parish that I've never seen before. We haven't had much chance to explore it."

"Wes has taken me to a few places, but he tends to be a creature of habit." Mary paused, then frowned. "Are you sure this is a good idea?"

"Well, we're not going to get out of the car. We're just going to see what he is up to." Suzie drove down the road that led to Parish. It was getting far more familiar to her as they had traveled it so often lately. Suzie took a sharp turn.

"Are we close?"

"Yes, it's just ahead. Sorry about that, I almost missed the turn." Suzie straightened the car then glanced at Mary. "You know, at some point, we're going to have to pick up the SUV."

"I know." Mary sighed as she tucked her phone back into her purse. "I've been trying not to think about it. We will have to find another mechanic to look at it. But it's not something that we have to do right away."

"No, you're right, it's not. Here we are." Suzie turned into the parking lot of a small restaurant. It looked more like an office space, but for the colorful sign that hung above the single, glass door.

"There he is, he's just coming out." Mary pointed to the man who descended three stone steps from the front door of the restaurant, then quickly lowered her hand. "Oops, I probably shouldn't point I guess."

"Whatever we can do to avoid drawing his attention is best, but I don't think that he saw you." Suzie eased the car into a parking spot. "We'll make it seem like we're going to park, and as soon as he gets to his car we'll be able to follow him."

"Uh oh, he's coming this way!" Mary gasped.

"Get down, if he sees us, he might recognize us." Suzie grabbed Mary's shoulder and pulled her down as she ducked down as well. In the quiet parking lot, they could both hear the sound of his footsteps as he approached. Suzie held her breath as she wondered if it was too late. Perhaps he had already spotted them, and now he would wonder why they were both crouched down inside the car.

Suzie ran through excuses in her mind as to why she had her head under her steering wheel. She hoped that he would turn in another direction, or be distracted by someone nearby. But the footsteps grew closer and closer. Despite the closed car door, each footfall struck Suzie's senses like a bomb exploding. She never expected him to be parked so close, but she hadn't bothered to sweep the parking lot to look for his car, either. It was a mistake that she didn't usually make. Now, she and Mary were about to face the consequences of it. As he neared the car, she held her breath. He walked right beside her, mere inches away, then she heard the footsteps continue past. They hadn't even slowed.

"I don't think he saw us." She peered across the car at Mary.

"Let's hope not." Mary eased her head up far enough to look in the passenger side mirror. "It looks like he's getting into his car." She straightened up a little further. "I think we're in the clear."

"That was close." Suzie sat up and ran her fingers through her shoulder-length hair. "Good thing we ducked."

"You've got way too much experience with this."

Mary flashed her a grin. "It's amazing how much I learn from you."

"From me?" Suzie raised an eyebrow, but kept her gaze fixated on Brennan. "Do you not recall the epic prom stakeout?"

"Oh that." Mary blushed and stared out through the windshield. "I wouldn't exactly call it a stakeout."

"You brought snacks, didn't you?" Suzie started to back the car out of the parking space as Brennan whipped out of the parking lot.

"Yes, yes I did." Mary turned another shade of red. "But it was necessary. My son's prom date wasn't to be trusted."

"Sure, sure." Suzie laughed as she followed behind Brennan. She left enough space for a car to slip in between her car and Brennan's. However, with the light traffic, no car did. As she hung back at a safe distance she wondered where Brennan might be headed next. It wasn't long before he turned into a bank. Suzie drove past it, around the block, and caught back up with Brennan's car as he exited the drive-through.

"So far there isn't much out of the ordinary." Mary frowned as they continued to follow Brennan through some residential streets.

"No, there isn't. But he may be trying to keep a low profile while the case is being investigated." Suzie slowed down as Brennan turned down a street with a name she recognized. "This is the street he lives on, isn't it?" She drove past.

"Yes, it is." Mary double-checked the information on her phone. "He must be on his way home."

"Let's come up from a different direction. We can park a few houses away and see if we can get a glimpse of what he's up to." Suzie turned down another side street.

"What happened to not getting out of the car?" Mary eyed her as she parked in front of a quiet house with an untended lawn.

"You don't have to get out of the car. Stay here, and I'll let you know if anything goes sideways."

"Ha, there's not much chance of that." Mary opened her door before Suzie could even step out. "If you're getting out, then I'm getting out, too."

"We're not going to talk to him, though. We're just going to take a look, that's all." Suzie met her eyes. "I don't want to take any chances."

"You're right, if he's the killer then he might not like having visitors, especially visitors he recognizes." Mary gazed at the house. "Maybe we can get a peek in a window."

"Let's find out." Suzie started along the side of the house and was just about to step on the driveway when Mary stopped her.

"Wait!" Mary pressed her hand against Suzie's shoulder and pushed her back a few steps. "He's not inside. He's in the garage." She put a finger to her lips.

Suzie nodded, and tried to peer around the corner of the garage. She could see that the door was open, and from the clanging sounds that drifted out through the door, she guessed that he was working on something. After a sharp curse, there was another clang, then Brennan emerged from the garage. He stalked towards the front door, and stepped inside. Suzie took the opportunity to peek inside the garage. Sunlight spilled into the garage and bounced off Brennan's race car.

"He's working on his car." Suzie frowned as she snapped a picture of it with her phone. "What kind of killer spends the afternoon working on his car?"

"One without remorse?" Mary's voice wavered some. "I'm not even convinced by that. But his casual attitude could just be a cover for what he did." She looked towards the front door at the sound of a subtle click. "Suzie, I think he's coming back." She grabbed her hand and tugged her back behind the garage. A second later Brennan headed down the front walkway to the garage door. He carried a bottle of beer in one hand, and a flashlight in the other.

As they leaned close to listen in on his activities, Mary's pocket began to ring. She gasped as she realized she hadn't turned the volume down on her phone. She fumbled for it, while Suzie tugged her away from the garage and past the neighbor's yard to the opposite side street towards her car.

"I'm so sorry, Suzie, I didn't even think about turning down my phone." She gulped down several breaths as she tried to steady her heartbeat and calm down.

"It's okay, Mary. I didn't turn down mine either. Some detectives we are." Suzie frowned and glanced over her shoulder. "If he heard it, I don't think he followed us."

"It was Carlene." Mary raised an eyebrow as she looked at her phone. "I should call her back."

"Go ahead, I don't think he spotted us. He probably didn't even hear the phone." Suzie eased the car into gear and pulled away from the side of the road slowly. If Brennan had noticed she didn't want him to see a car tearing away from the curb, that would certainly gain his attention. As she began to drive, she glanced over at Mary, who had the phone up to her ear.

"Carlene? Sorry I missed your call."

"Mary, I didn't know who else to call. You're not going to believe this!"

"What is it?" Mary gestured for Suzie to listen as she pressed the speaker phone button.

"Brennan just threatened me! He showed up at my house, I didn't even know he knew where I lived. He pounded on the door until I opened it. I wasn't going to, but he kept knocking so hard. When I answered it, he shouted at me, and told me if I said anything about what happened to Graham, he would come back to shut me up for good!" Carlene gasped out her words. Her voice wavered as she took another heavy breath. "I'm so scared, Mary."

CHAPTER 13

Mary's heart pounded against her chest. She would have believed the fear in Carlene's voice, had it not been for the fact that she and Suzie had been following Brennan for quite some time. Carlene was a very good actress, she managed to sound terrified, when Mary was sure every word she said was a lie.

"I'm so sorry that happened." Mary met Suzie's eyes briefly, before Suzie turned her eyes back to the road. "Is he still there, now?"

"No, he left a few minutes ago. I would call the cops, but I just can't risk it. Do you think you could let the detective know? I'm sure he'll be able to track Brennan down." Her voice evened out as she continued. "I never would have thought he was capable of this, but clearly he is."

"Are you safe, now?" Mary did her best to sound concerned. But she was more shocked than concerned. Not only had Carlene concocted this story, but she wanted to draw herself and Suzie into it, along with Wes. It seemed to her that Carlene's intention was to put the focus of the investigation on Brennan.

"Yes." Her voice shuddered. "If I ever have to see him again I think I might die from fear. He's such a nasty man."

"I'm so sorry you went through that. Brennan does seem to have a temper. Make sure you stay safe." Mary looked over at Suzie, who shook her head as she narrowed her eyes. "Why don't we come to check on you? We could stay with you until Wes finds Brennan."

"No, it's okay. I feel safe now I know the police will be looking for him. Have you seen Marlin? Is he still staying there at Dune House?" Her voice grew more urgent with every word she spoke.

"No, he left last night." Mary frowned. "Why? Did you see him today, too?"

"No, I didn't see him, but I want to. I've been trying to get in contact with him. I really need to speak to him." Her voice wavered again. "Any idea where he might be?"

"What do you need to speak to him about?" Mary glanced over at Suzie. "Did he threaten you, again?"

"Please, I just need to speak to Marlin. If you see him, please let him know that."

"I will. But I'd still like to meet with you. Suzie and I have a few things we want to talk to you about, and we want to make sure that you're doing okay. How about tonight? Can we meet up tonight?"

"Sure, I guess. Where?"

"Maybe at the garage? I need to get the SUV if possible. I know it's insensitive, but I do need to try to get it fixed." Mary hesitated as she wondered how Carlene might react to that.

"It's okay, we can meet there. I know where the keys are. Graham did finish fixing it, though. I was writing up the invoice for it that morning. I was about to call you when everything happened." Carlene sighed.

"He finished it?" Mary looked at Suzie with amazement.

"Yes, he started it straight after you dropped it off, he wanted it to be done for you as quickly as possible. He seemed to like both of you. He mentioned Dune House, and how many people he'd heard say good things about it. I'm sure he did a good job."

"Thank you for sharing that with us." Mary pressed her hand to her chest. "Around seven tonight at the garage?"

"Yes, I'll be there. Apparently, Graham had a silent partner in the garage. He is going to get new mechanics in to run the place. So, I'm getting things ready for him. But remember, if you see Marlin, I need him to get in contact with me as soon as possible." She hung up the phone before Mary could say another word.

As Mary lowered her phone, she sighed. "So, now we know for sure that Carlene is a liar, and a good one."

"Yes, we do." Suzie frowned as she turned towards Garber.

"I can't believe that she would make up a story like that. Honestly, if we hadn't just been following Brennan I would have one hundred percent believed her." Mary shook her head as she sunk down in her seat. "Some detective I am."

"Carlene is likely a member of a gang. Honest people don't exactly join gangs. I'm sure she has a natural talent for lying." Suzie turned down the road that led to Dune House. "Besides, she had me fooled as well. She plays the sweet, innocent victim pretty well."

"But why is she playing it?" Mary gazed out at the water that sparkled blue in the glare of the sunlight. "Do you think she's trying to frame Brennan for the murder? Do you think she's trying to protect someone?"

"I don't know exactly. Maybe she realized that Wes and Jason know about her connection to the gang. We know that Marlin knew, and he was threatening her with that information. Marlin suspected she was trying to protect Brody. Yes, he has an alibi, but maybe he found a way to fake it. If so, Carlene may be trying to protect him. Maybe she thinks if she points the spotlight more towards Brennan, the heat will ease up on Brody."

"Maybe."

"Or maybe she knows that Brennan did this and she is trying to get him arrested to protect herself." She pulled into the parking lot, then looked over at Mary. "Or maybe she really was involved in the murder and she's doing everything she can to throw Wes off her trail."

"It's possible. But she was attacked, too. What

about the bruise? You've seen the huge bruise. She must have been hit with something very heavy. Do you really think she would do that to herself?" Mary winced at the thought and then stepped out of the car. A warm breeze blew off the water and soothed the tension in her face.

"It's a good way to cover up her involvement, but from the look of that bruise I don't think she could do that to herself." Suzie headed up the porch to the front door of Dune House. "Maybe it's the person she is protecting? Maybe she has a partner?"

"Oh, I hadn't thought of that." Mary narrowed her eyes. "It's possible, though. Maybe someone from the gang? But what is her motive for killing Graham? Maybe he found out that she had been involved in a gang?"

"I don't think she'd need to kill him over that. He could have just fired her, or she could have quit. But maybe Graham confronted her about it. Maybe he wanted to try to help her? Maybe someone else from the gang wanted to keep him quiet?" Suzie cringed as she opened the door and stepped inside. "It's hard to think that he might have been killed for trying to steer her in the right direction."

"It's also a big leap to make. Everyone said

Graham was such a good and honest guy, but what if he was involved in the car thefts?"

"I don't know, it's just an endless sea of 'what ifs'." Suzie dropped the keys on the dining room table and sighed. "I feel like we haven't gotten any closer to the truth. Brennan is still a suspect, Brody is still a suspect, and now Carlene is definitely a suspect, and there's always the loose end of Marlin. He came here for a reason, the only problem is we don't know exactly what that reason was."

"You're right." Mary pulled out a chair at the dining room table and sat down.

"Maybe Brody is telling the truth. Maybe he really was at that class. Do you think that Carlene and Brennan could have been working together? Maybe that's why she's turning on him now?"

"Interesting." Mary considered the possibility as she pursed her lips. "But if that's the case, why is she so desperate to see Marlin? You know, he's the mystery factor in all of this. We know about Carlene's connection to the gang, we know about Brennan's anger towards Graham because of his damaged race car, we know that Brody might be connected to the gang as well. What we don't know is exactly how Marlin is involved in all of this, there are so many questions around him."

"The great mystery, maybe it's time we found out a little bit more about him." Suzie rapped her knuckles lightly on the table. "Of all of our suspects, he would certainly know how to commit a crime and get away with it."

"True, and he might even have the right connections with active law enforcement officers to smooth anything over that comes up in the investigation. His former captain is singing his praises. But that doesn't exactly jive with the man we saw pointing a gun at Carlene, does it?"

"No, it doesn't." Suzie pulled out her phone and opened a web browser. "Now we know his real name, maybe we can dig up a little bit more about him. Are you going to call Wes about what Carlene said?"

"Not just yet. I want to figure out what she's up to first. I'm not going to let her manipulate me that way. We know that she is up to something, that's for sure. We just don't know if it's because she's innocent and trying to protect herself, or if she's trying to protect someone and is possibly even involved in the murder." Mary rubbed her hand along her forehead. "The problem is we really have no idea what is going on. Is it Carlene who is playing a game? Is it Marlin?"

"We haven't seen or heard from him since he left Dune House." Suzie frowned as she scrolled through a few things the search returned about Marlin.

"Well, I didn't expect we would. We didn't exactly end things on the best terms."

"You're right about that." Suzie stood up and began to pace back and forth. "But I am still not convinced that he didn't have something to do with this. He conveniently shows up right before the murder takes place? He says he's a hired private investigator, but what if his employer paid him a little extra?" She paused and looked straight into Mary's eyes. "What if he is also an assassin?"

"I hadn't considered that." Mary took a sharp breath at the thought. "I guess that is possible. We know that he went there the day before Graham was killed. What was to stop him from following through with his employer's wishes?"

"His employer, who we still don't know the name of, that's the problem. I think we need to speak to him, and get a better feel for why Marlin was even here in the first place." She began to pace again. "But we're not going to be able to find that out unless we find Marlin."

"I know Wes told him not to leave town." Mary

crossed her arms as she considered the possibilities. "There aren't too many other places he could be staying, at least here in Garber."

"Or eating!" Suzie snapped her fingers. "I gave him coupons and a menu to the diner when he first arrived. Maybe we should check and see if he's been there?"

"I'll give Pam a call. I bet she's working." Mary dialed the number of the waitress she'd become friends with since moving to Garber.

"Hello, this is Pam."

"Hi Pam, this is Mary. Sorry to bother you. Are you working right now?"

"Yes, I am. But it's no bother. We're not too busy."

"Do you know James? He was staying here at Dune House?"

"Sure, why?"

"We're just trying to locate him." Mary frowned as she wondered if Pam might be in any danger around him. "Could you let me know if he comes in?"

"He's here now." Her voice lowered some as she spoke into the phone. "He just ordered his meal. Do you want me to stall him until you get here?"

"Yes, that would be great. Thanks." Mary hung

up the phone, then turned to face Suzie. "He's at the diner, he just ordered his food. If we get there now we should be able to speak to him."

"Let's go." Suzie grabbed her purse. "I'm starving anyway."

"Me, too." Mary grabbed her purse as well and headed for the door. On the way to the car she checked on Pilot and hesitated as she saw him curled up in his soft bed in the yard. For some reason she had the urge to bring him with her. Instead, she pushed the thought away and headed after Suzie.

Suzie drove the short distance to the diner. As she turned into the parking lot she felt some relief that she'd managed to make it there without facing any disasters.

Together, they entered the diner, which was filled with hungry customers.

"There!" Mary hissed to Suzie, then tugged her forward some. "Near the back."

"Yes, I see him."

"What's the plan?" Mary started to ask, but Suzie walked boldly past her towards Marlin's table. Mary hurried to catch up with her.

"You two." Marlin looked up from his plate with

a slow smirk. "I suppose you're going to tell me that this is a coincidence?"

"No coincidence." Suzie pulled a chair up to his table and sat down. "Mary and I were looking for you."

"Please, join me." He chuckled and gestured to the free chair across from him. "Sit down, Mary."

Mary's skin prickled as she eased her way down into the chair. Was she sitting down across from a murderer?

"Thanks for the invite." Suzie locked eyes with him to let him know that she intended to be in control of the conversation. "We need some more information from you, Marlin."

"You do?" He eyed her. "What kind of information?"

"The kind that tells us who your employer is." Mary took over, as her desire to know the truth came to the surface. "Who hired you to come here?"

"I'm sorry, that information is confidential. Ah, there's Pam. Would you like to order something?" His eyes sparkled as he looked between them.

"How can you be enjoying this?" Suzie stared at him as anger bristled every nerve in her body. "A good man is dead."

"First, I'm not enjoying anyone being dead.

Second, I'm not so sure he was a good man. Are you?" Marlin picked up his fork and pushed some of his mashed potatoes around on his plate. "Last, the two of you continue to bark up the wrong tree. Why is that? Because I'm not from around here?" He scooped up some of the potatoes. The gummy white concoction dripped slowly through the tines of the fork as he stared at them. "Or is it just because you don't like me?"

"Marlin, you lied to us from the first moment you arrived." Suzie's voice was sharpened by her frustration. "And now you're showing us that you don't want to make the slightest effort to help us."

"Help you what?" He set the fork down again, the bite of potatoes abandoned. "Set me up?"

"Why would you think that?" Suzie leaned forward to take a closer look into his eyes.

"Why not? You reported me to the police about the gun, you threw me out of Dune House, and now for some reason that I don't understand, you are obsessed with getting me to violate my employer's privacy. I've told you on multiple occasions, I had nothing to do with this, and yet you continue to come at me as if I'm a suspect." Marlin rocked back in his chair and folded his hands together across his stomach. "Perhaps I have the wrong idea here, but

I'm fairly certain that you would like to see me behind bars."

"All we want is the truth." Suzie looked into his eyes. "The less information you give us, the less chance there is of us finding out the truth."

"Or your version of the truth?" Marlin pushed his plate aside. "Let's say I told you the name of my employer, and you decided to go after him or confront him. Do you think I would ever be able to get another paying job? Do you think, even though I'm innocent, that I will be able to live down the consequences of divulging my employer's information, and continue to have a career?" He shook his head as he studied their stunned faces. "No, you're not the least bit concerned about that, because it isn't your problem. And, ladies so sorry to tell you, your need for information isn't my problem." He stood up from the table, tossed down some cash, and headed for the door.

CHAPTER 14

Marlin's absence left them both in silence for some time. Then Mary shifted in her chair. The subtle squeak of the chair leg against the tiled floor startled both of them out of their dazed state.

"Well, that didn't go well." Suzie frowned as she looked over at Mary.

"I didn't expect him to tell us, really." Mary sighed as she settled back in her chair. "He's a clever man."

"Too clever." Suzie glanced up as Pam walked over to them.

"Would you two like to order? I can clear this all away." She began to pile up Marlin's dishes.

"Yes, actually. We need to eat, Suzie." Mary met

her eyes. "Then we can decide what our next step will be."

"Good idea." Suzie's stomach rumbled as she spoke.

After a quick lunch, Suzie drove them back to Dune House.

"I have an idea." She turned towards Mary as they stepped out of the car.

"You do?"

"Marlin said his client hired Graham to repair some cars. Maybe he sells them?"

"Maybe." Mary nodded.

"You know that new high-end place in Parish that everyone talks about because it's so out of place."

"Kline Automobiles?" Mary snapped her fingers. "Of course. Let's go there now."

"I think we should see if we can find out a bit about the owner first. What do you think?"

"Okay, let's do some research."

They rushed into Dune House and let Pilot inside. He was so excited to see them and even more excited about his food. After feeding him they sat down at the dining room table as Suzie started searching. It was easy to find the information.

"Benjamin Kline is the owner." Suzie nodded.

Suzie and Mary turned towards the front door as it opened, and Jason walked in.

"Jason!" Suzie greeted him.

"Hi ladies. I just wanted to check on you. Make sure you aren't getting in any trouble." He smiled as he looked between them.

"No, nothing to report." Suzie shook her head. "But we were wondering if you know anything about Benjamin Kline, the owner of Kline Automobiles in Parish."

"All I know is that you need to steer clear of him." Jason's expression darkened.

"What do you mean? Have you met him?" Suzie asked.

"No, I've never met him. He's only new to the area, but I know that he sells very high-end cars. We're talking about cars I would never be able to own." He shook his head as he straightened his shoulders. "He's not someone you want to get on the wrong side of from what I understand. He's not someone to be toyed with."

"Okay," Suzie said.

"You haven't seen Marlin? Have you?" Jason asked.

"We have, actually." Suzie nodded. "At the diner, about thirty minutes ago. Why, were you looking for him?"

"Yes. We got a call that he's been harassing Carlene. Wes asked us to keep a look out for him here in Garber. Any idea where he went after that?" He pulled out his phone.

"No, sorry." Mary frowned. "I wouldn't fully believe everything Carlene says. I don't think she is completely trustworthy." She briefly explained that Carlene had called her about Brennan. She left out a few details so that Jason wouldn't know that they had been following Brennan. She knew if he knew, he would have been furious.

"Okay, that's interesting, at least we know Marlin is in town. Thanks." He hurried out the door and down the steps towards his patrol car.

"Well, that settles it, I guess." Mary gazed after him. "We're never going to find anything out from Benjamin Kline."

"He'll only hide if he thinks we're after information. I have an idea." Suzie stood up and looked directly at Mary. "Put on your finest dress. You and I are in the market for a car worth more than everything we've ever owned combined."

"Great idea!" Mary laughed as she headed for her room.

After Suzie dressed, she knocked lightly on Mary's bedroom door.

"Can I see what you've picked out?"

"Sure, come on in." Mary turned to face her.

"No, that's not going to do." Suzie walked slowly around Mary and swept her gaze over the long dress she wore. "You look like you're going to a funeral, not shopping for a new car."

"Suzie." Mary sighed as she flopped her hands against the skirt of her dress. "You know I have no idea how to do any of this. But this is the best dress that I have. It's not like I'm going to fit into anything of yours." She patted her belly. "You've never been this size."

"Mary, you're gorgeous. The dress is pretty, but not for what we're doing today. I think we can come up with something. Let me just take a look." She stepped around her and into her closet. As she sorted through the clothing she began to see the colors and styles come together. Soon she had an outfit for Mary to try on.

"That blouse and those pants together?" Mary scrunched up her nose. "Don't you think that's a little showy?"

"I think it will look gorgeous on you." Suzie

thrust the hangers towards her. "Now change quickly, we want to get there before he closes up for the day."

"All right, fine I will. But I'm still not sure about this." She frowned as Suzie headed out the door of her room.

"Just put it on, trust me." Suzie closed the door behind her, then checked her make-up in the hall mirror. She didn't usually wear much, but on this occasion she'd gone a little heavy. They needed to look the part if they hoped to get any information from him. Jason's warning echoed through her mind. Just how dangerous of a man could Benjamin Kline be?

〜

*I*t was quite a drive to get to Kline's high-end dealership, which gave them both some time to rehearse their roles.

"I'm not sure I can pull this off, Suzie." Mary smoothed down her blouse. "I've never been wealthy, I've never even had more than I needed."

"It's not so hard. Just remember, you have enough in your purse to buy whatever you please."

"I've never experienced that." Mary laughed. "But I guess I can pretend."

"Don't worry, we can handle this." Suzie turned into the parking lot of a large building with several glass walls. It wasn't hard to see the flashy cars through the glass as they were all brightly colored and aimed towards the outside.

"Let's do this." Mary shot Suzie a brief, nervous look, then stepped out of the car.

"It's almost closing time, I doubt there will be any other customers inside." Suzie stepped out of the car as well. "We need to put some distance between us and this car or he's never going to believe we're well off enough to step inside his showroom." She caught Mary's elbow and drew her along beside her. As they reached the towering glass door, it swung open to reveal a tall, fit man wearing a well-tailored suit.

"Welcome." He smiled as he held open the door for both of them. "I wasn't expecting another appointment today. Did you have a chance to schedule one?"

"No, I'm sorry, we didn't." Suzie smiled at him and offered her most endearing laugh. "My friend, Mary is in the market for a car. When she told me this, I just knew I had to refer her here. I window shop your cars all the time. I've never been daring enough to come inside, but Mary, she's a lot braver than I am."

"Is that so?" He smiled as he turned his attention to Mary. "I guess you know a good thing when you see it."

"I do." Mary clutched her purse, but did her best to keep her voice smooth. "I'm interested in something very reliable, and of course with all of the bells and whistles. I do like my little luxuries."

"As you should." He offered her his arm. "Can I get you both some coffee? Tea?"

"Nothing for me, thanks." Mary swept her gaze over the assortment of vehicles lined up in the showroom. She'd never laid her eyes on most of them.

"She'd just like to look at a few, I think. We wouldn't want her to get overwhelmed." Suzie patted the curve of Mary's shoulder, then eased her in the direction of a cherry red sportscar. "This one looks like it would suit you just fine."

"Hmm, it seems a little bright." Mary leaned close to peer through the window of the front driver's side door.

"You don't have to look from afar, go on and get inside." Benjamin reached past her to open the door.

"Oh no, thank you." Mary stepped back as she

imagined trying to bend the right way to get into the car. Her knees were not likely to cooperate. "What about this one?" She started towards another car in the showroom.

"Perhaps before we try any out, we could find out a little bit more about you, Benjamin." Suzie turned to face him, his gaze was focused on Mary. He glanced at her, then raised an eyebrow.

"I don't recall introducing myself." He stared at her, the question in his eyes quite evident.

"No, you didn't. You must be off your game tonight." Suzie smiled and casually glanced at Mary, before looking back at him. "No matter, I already know who you are. Benjamin Kline. Did you know Graham from Graham's Garage?"

"Wait a minute." His hands balled into fists at his sides. "Is this some kind of sting? Are you the police?"

"No, we're not the police." Mary walked over to join her. "But we do want to know the truth about Graham's death. Did you know him?"

"Not in person." He frowned, then glanced at his watch. "I have nothing to say to either of you, I'm going to call my lawyer if you continue to harass me."

"We're not harassing you, we just want to know if you know anything about Graham." Suzie nodded, and offered him a confident smile.

"This is ridiculous, I know nothing about what happened to him." He took a step back.

"You're right, we don't belong here." Mary met his eyes as she interrupted him. "I will never be able to afford a car like this. But I will spend every ounce of my energy to find out what happened to Graham. Do you want to fight that battle, or do you want to give us a little information?"

"I don't want any trouble. I've got nothing to hide." He shoved his hands into his pockets and stared at both of them. "What do you want to know?"

"You said you didn't know Graham in person, what does that mean?" Suzie locked eyes with him.

"It means that we talked now and then. I have a few customers in Parish, and a few more in Garber. We don't have a service department on site and they don't like traveling far for their service. So, I arranged with Graham for him to work on their cars. He came highly recommended. Then my customers' cars started getting stolen. As you can imagine, I was not pleased." He shrugged.

"Not pleased, or enraged?" Mary studied him. "Just how angry did it make you that somehow your customers were being robbed, and it was likely your fault?"

"I don't like what you're implying. I asked someone to look into this matter for the sake of my customers. Of course, I wanted to know what happened. My customers invest a lot of money in these vehicles, and part of their draw is the state-of-the-art security that goes with them. I think that somehow the keys were being cloned and I wanted to know how that was happening and who was doing it."

"Cloning?" Suzie asked.

"Yes, thieves clone the frequencies from the keys. So yes, I wanted to know how the cars were being stolen. But I wouldn't have done anything to harm anyone. I'm a businessman, that's it." He looked between them. "Now, if that's all, it's time to close up. You two have a nice night." He walked back over to the door.

"One more thing." Suzie followed after him. "What do you know about Brody and Carlene?"

"Brody? Carlene?" Benjamin blinked, then shook his head. "I've never heard of them. Last chance to leave without me calling the authorities." He held open the door for them.

"Okay, sorry to have bothered you." Mary nodded.

"Goodnight, Mr. Kline." Suzie gestured for Mary to step out ahead of her.

CHAPTER 15

On the drive back to Garber, Suzie and Mary discussed their meeting with Benjamin.

"I honestly don't think he had a clue what Marlin was up to. He didn't seem to recognize Brody or Carlene's names at all." Mary frowned as she wove the car in and out of the traffic build-up that came with rush hour. "Why do you think Marlin kept threatening Carlene? She could be lying about it, but if he is still threatening her he has to know something we don't, something more than just her gang affiliation."

"I don't know, but I intend to find out. Pam told me he mentioned that he's staying at the Bluebird, just outside of Garber. I say, we make one more try to get information out of him."

"Are you sure?" Mary gazed through the windshield of the car. "It's getting late, and we're supposed to meet with Carlene, remember?"

"Oh, I remember, that's why I want to talk to Marlin first. Here's the hotel, the next right." She pointed out a sign on the road. Suzie quickly sent a text to Paul explaining that she might be a little late for dinner as they were planning on picking up the car that night.

"I see it." Mary turned into the parking lot of the Bluebird Motel. For a low-cost motel, it managed to keep its grounds clean, but its customers were another story. It was known for hosting seedy characters. "There he is." Mary pointed to a motel room as Marlin exited it. She watched him get into the driver's side of a car. There was a large sticker advertising the rental company in the rear windshield. "A rental car."

"Oh, he's backing out," Suzie said. Mary followed behind him as he pulled into a grocery store parking lot. The parking lot was almost full. After driving down a few aisles, Marlin parked in a spot. "Pull in there."

"Okay." Mary pulled into a spot a few spots away from Marlin's.

"What's he doing?" Suzie asked as they stared towards his car.

"It looks like he's just sitting there," Mary said. "Oh, he's pulling out now."

"Weird, he didn't even get out of the car." Suzie frowned. "Keep your distance so he doesn't spot you."

"All right, I'll hang back. Then we can get behind him." Mary drummed her fingertips on the steering wheel as she slowed down. Marlin's car came into view, she waited a few more seconds to be sure that he wouldn't spot them. However, as she watched him continue through the parking lot, her eyes widened. "Isn't that Carlene's car?"

"Where?" Suzie sat forward in her seat and peered through the windshield. The crowded grocery store parking lot was full of cars on the move, but it only took her a few seconds to spot Carlene's car. It was right in front of Marlin's. "Oh wow, yes I think it is. Do you think he's following her?"

"He doesn't seem to be the type to let things slide, so I'd guess yes, he is." Mary frowned as she slowed down a little more. "Should we keep following him?"

"Sure. It kills two birds with one stone, right? Besides, I don't want Marlin to have the chance to point his gun at her again. I still don't trust him, and at this point, he might be after her more out of revenge than because of a job." Suzie glanced towards the stoplight at the end of the parking lot. "It looks like they are planning to go left. Hang back some and let a few other cars get between you and Marlin, otherwise we'll all be lined up together and I'm sure we'll be spotted."

"Okay." Mary took a deep breath and turned down an aisle of the parking lot, away from Marlin's car. She wound her way back through to the exit, once a few other cars had piled up in the left turn lane. As she turned on her turn signal she glanced over at Suzie. "Maybe you should drive?"

"It's too late for that." Suzie pointed to the green arrow that popped up on the stoplight. "We're going. You can do this. All you have to do is drive, I will keep track of where Marlin is going."

As Mary wound through the streets after the two cars, she realized they were getting far away from Garber, and Parish.

"They're headed into the mountains." Mary

glanced over at Suzie. "I've never really driven up there before."

"It's all right, I'm sure they're not going to get too far before they turn in another direction." Suzie stared hard through the windshield. To her surprise, Marlin began to wind his way up the mountain. She hadn't driven on the mountain much either. There was never a need to. But she'd heard stories about the treacherous roads. It was an unincorporated area, and neither town wanted to claim ownership and tackle the repairs that the roads needed.

Mary continued along the road with some space between her car and Marlin's. The road wasn't very populated.

"Do you think he will notice us? I mean, he must."

"I think he's too preoccupied with following Carlene to suspect that anyone is following him. But he's speeding up." Suzie frowned.

"I'm not going to lose him." Mary increased her speed. As she did the wheels of the car bounced through some potholes and uneven patches on the road.

"Mary, slow down!" Suzie braced her hands against the dashboard as the road became even more uneven. "Something isn't right, slow down!"

"Okay, I'm trying." Mary frowned as she pressed her foot against the brake. "It's the slope of the road, it's making it hard to control the car." She looked over at Suzie and caught sight of the fear in her eyes. She wished Suzie was driving, she was much more confident than her. "It's okay, I've got it. Just hold on!" Mary pressed down harder on the brake and held the wheel steady as the car shuddered in response to the sudden pressure. Ahead of them, Marlin seemed to be having more trouble. The rear of his car slid back and forth, then the front aimed towards the edge of the narrow road.

"Oh no!" Suzie gasped as she saw Marlin's car head for the edge. "He's going to go over!"

"Maybe not, maybe he'll just—" Mary let out a short scream as the front wheels of Marlin's car tipped over the edge of the road. "We have to do something!"

"Focus on the road, Mary!" Suzie grabbed the steering wheel as the car began to drift towards the edge as well. "There's nothing we can do! It's too late." Her voice trembled as her words were punctuated by the grind and squeal of Marlin's car as it continued over the rim of the cliff.

Tears blurred Mary's vision with panic, as she pushed the brake harder. Finally, the car came to a stop. She threw the car door open and jumped out, with Suzie only a few steps behind her. As Mary ran towards the cliff, she noticed that Carlene's car continued on. It didn't even look like it had slowed down.

"Should we go try and help him?" Suzie moved towards the edge of the cliff. She could barely take a breath as her heart pounded and the world around her spun. Had she just witnessed the end of a man's life? She hoped it wasn't true, but she knew that it very likely was.

"No, Suzie don't." Mary caught her by the elbow and pulled her back towards her. "We need to call for help. We don't know what caused Marlin to lose control. It could have been an oil patch, or it could have been the slope or — "

"Or someone could have tampered with his car." Suzie narrowed her eyes at the thought. As her heart began to slow, she could think clearly again, and immediately she realized how strange it was that Carlene continued on. There was no chance that she hadn't seen Marlin slide off the road. She was only a few feet ahead of him when it happened. In fact, she must have sped up in order to avoid a collision. Had she known it was Marlin? "Oh Mary, what if Carlene really had something to do with this?"

"We have no proof." Mary lowered the phone in her hand. "I just called Wes. He said help is on the way. Jason is coming, too." She wiped a hand across her forehead and looked back at the edge of the cliff. "Maybe if it wasn't so steep, we could find a way down there."

"No." Suzie breathed. "Don't even think it, Mary. You were right, it's far too dangerous."

"I know it is." Mary winced as she did her best to hold back her tears. "But Suzie —"

"I know, sweetheart." Suzie wrapped her arms around her and held her close. "I know, it's just terrible, but there is nothing that we can do now. We called for help, and hopefully they will get here quickly. Let's go back to the car. It's safer there." She led Mary back to the car. Sirens screamed through the balmy evening air.

~

The next few minutes were a blur of flashing lights, endless sirens, and uniforms. Minutes later, Wes' car pulled up, followed closely by Jason's patrol car. The narrow mountain road, barren not long before, was now spotted with large, bright vehicles. The headlights of all of the vehicles gave the area an ambient glow.

"Mary!" Wes ran towards the car, just as Mary stepped out of it.

"Wes, we're both okay." She looked over her shoulder at Suzie. "Marlin's car went over the edge. There are rescuers down there, but no one has come back up."

"It doesn't look good." Suzie crossed her arms as she looked past Wes towards Jason. "It's such a sheer drop."

"No, it doesn't." Jason paused beside them. "What happened?"

"It looked like he just lost control." Mary frowned. "Our car was slipping on the road, too. But it was like he couldn't slow down."

Wes stepped aside to speak briefly into his radio. As he did, between the crackle of the connection, Mary tried to hear what they were saying, but she couldn't hear anything. She turned towards Suzie, whose expression indicated she was trying to do the same thing.

"Looks like he's going to be okay. A few injuries, of course, but it looks like he's going to be fine."

Wes walked back towards them. "Luckily, it's a rescue."

"Are you okay?" Jason asked.

"It's just such a relief." Suzie sighed.

"I'm sorry, I have to investigate this. How did all of you end up on this road?" Wes looked into Mary's eyes.

"We were following him." Mary's cheeks flushed. "But I didn't get close to him."

"Was he running from you?" Wes' expression tensed.

"No, he wasn't. He was following Carlene." Mary glanced over at Suzie, who nodded. "When we started to follow him, we realized that he was following Carlene. Or at least a car that we've seen in Carlene's driveway. We couldn't see who was driving it. When his car went off the road, her car just kept going."

"Who else would be driving her car?" Jason raised an eyebrow. "Maybe they didn't see the crash?" He frowned, and Wes briefly met his eyes. The road was on the border of Parish and Garber. Was Marlin's accident a part of Wes' investigation, or a new investigation for Jason? The two would have to figure it out.

"Can we go, Jason?" Suzie asked. "We're both exhausted."

"Yes, you should." Jason nodded.

"I'll be by the house later to take your statements. Do you want me to have someone drive you? You've had quite a shock," Wes said.

"It's all right, I can drive." Suzie glanced around at the flashing lights once more. It was hard to believe that the mountain road was ever dim.

Wes gave Mary a quick hug, he tended to remain professional, but his strong arms around her were an elixir for the anxiety that she felt. Once they were back in the car, Suzie carefully turned the car around and headed back down the mountain.

"This isn't the way to Dune House." Mary frowned as Suzie made a left turn at the base of the mountain.

"We're going to find Carlene." Suzie shot a brief look in her direction. "The officers are too occupied to find her right now. She will have some time to either run, or cover up what she did."

"You think she did something to Marlin's car?" Mary's eyes widened at the thought.

"Yes, I do. I think she knew he was following her and that she led him up that mountain on purpose. But I want to find out for sure."

"But how are we going to find her?" Mary settled back in the passenger seat.

"My guess is she'll be heading back to her house, likely to attempt to create an alibi for herself. She probably had no idea that we were following after Marlin." Suzie turned down another road. "We're almost there. If we don't catch her there, then I'm not sure where she might have gone."

"And what are we going to do when we do catch her?" Mary peered through the fading light at Suzie. "Are we going to accuse her of sabotaging Marlin's car?"

"I'm not sure, yet." Suzie frowned.

"If she did try to kill Marlin, then she could have killed Graham, too." Mary glanced at her phone as it buzzed. "It's a text from Wes. He said it looks like the brake lines in Marlin's car were cut. Apparently, he's only had that rental a day or two, but he would have known right away if the brake lines were damaged when he picked it up."

"Someone must have done it before Marlin started following Carlene. Which means she probably knew that she had a tail." Suzie turned down Carlene's street. "Do you think she did it to stop him from sharing whatever information he had about her? He was blackmailing her in a sense."

"Maybe. Or maybe she thought he knew more than he did. We need to be careful."

Suzie parked the car across the street from Carlene's small house. Right away she noticed two cars in the driveway. One was Carlene's, the other was an unfamiliar car. Before she could even point it out, a man stepped out through the front door. He wore thick boots, jeans, and an old, white t-shirt.

"Who is that?" Suzie narrowed her eyes. As he approached his car, the outside light turned on, and revealed the tattoo on his forearm. The same as Carlene's.

Mary concentrated on his face and noticed his familiar features. Her mind flashed back to that day at the garage, as Graham tossed him the keys.

"It's Brody!" She gasped at the sight of him. "Marlin might have been right. What if he was the one that was driving Carlene's car? What if Carlene was protecting him?"

"If he was ruthless enough to try to kill Marlin, then he might have killed Graham, too." Suzie started the car as he pulled out of the driveway. "Let's see where he's going."

Mary slouched down in her seat. She wasn't sure about following another car, but the draw of finding Graham's killer was too much to resist.

"He's going so fast." Suzie frowned as she tried to keep up with the way the man wove through the neighborhood, sticking to smaller streets, and avoiding the main roads. When he finally did pull out on the highway that ran between Garber and Parish, he blended into thick traffic. Suzie tried to keep her eye on him, but the sun had set, and the darkness combined with the glare of multiple sets of headlights made it impossible. "Oh no, I've lost him." She sighed as she stopped at a red light, and the cars ahead of them continued to move forward.

"It's all right, Suzie. Now we know that Carlene was under the thumb of a very dangerous man. It's likely that Brody killed Graham, and then Carlene was too scared to tell the truth." Mary glanced at the time on the clock on the radio. "We're supposed to be meeting her at the garage soon. Maybe she'll be headed there soon. Why don't we go check on Pilot then head there?"

"Good idea." Suzie nodded. "But, Mary you need to keep in mind that Carlene was probably involved in all of this. Maybe she's protecting Brody because she's scared of him. She might have even protected him because she's in love with him. Remember those boots you tripped over on our first visit?"

"Oh my." Mary's eyes widened. "He might have been there the whole time."

"And she never said a word." Suzie narrowed her eyes.

"I'm going to text Wes the license plate of that car, maybe he will be able to find him." Mary added in all the details she could think of in the text, then set her phone down. Hopefully, he would be able to catch Brody before he had a chance to disappear.

CHAPTER 16

*A*fter stopping at Dune House to make sure that Pilot was fed, and everything was okay they went to the garage to hopefully meet Carlene.

When Suzie and Mary pulled up to Graham's Garage the parking lot was empty, but for the cars parked along the side of the property, one of which was the SUV. Mary's eyes lingered on it for a moment. It seemed like ages ago that she'd bought it and dropped it off with Graham, but it had really only been a few days.

"Do you think Carlene is there?" Mary peered out through the windshield. "It looks completely dark."

"I don't see her car, but it could be behind the

garage, I guess." Suzie glanced around the parking lot. "I could send her a text and see if she responds. It might give us an idea if she's intending to come."

"No, don't." Mary looked back at the garage. "If we want a chance to snoop around, this is it. Maybe we can find some evidence that will prove that Brody is linked to all of this." She shook her head slowly. "Honestly, it's still hard for me to believe that Carlene was involved in Graham's murder. I don't know why, after we witnessed Marlin going off the road. If that was her driving I know she's capable of anything. But still, I can't quite wrap my head around it." She sighed.

"She did come off as quite nice. It's difficult to believe she'd let someone hurt her like that if she was in on it. I still think it's possible that Brody killed Graham without Carlene's knowledge. She might not even know that Brody's the one who knocked her out. But one thing has been bothering me, why was her bruise so dark? It was apparently fresh, but it looked so dark. I still don't understand why she would implicate Brennan. To try to keep the focus off her maybe? Maybe we're off base and she knows Brennan did it. But you're right, we should take a look around." Suzie turned the car off and tucked her keys into her pocket.

"But how are we going to get in? It's not like we have a key."

"Maybe there's something open, a window, or the back door. I say we take a look, it can't hurt, right?" Suzie popped open the car door before Mary could answer her. She was going to have a look, no matter what. As she approached the garage, she heard Mary fall into step behind her.

"It does look empty." Mary peered through one of the dark windows.

"I don't think she's here, yet."

"If she's planning to come at all." Mary frowned as she walked the perimeter of the garage. "After what happened today she might have taken off."

"Do you really think she had something to do with Marlin's accident?" Suzie followed after her.

"I think it's possible. She's worked in the garage long enough to know how to sabotage a car, and obviously Brody would know how. Someone cut his brakes, there's no question about that. Who else would do something like that? Here." She pushed on a long window and felt it ease up along the frame. "Can you fit through there?" She looked over at Suzie.

"Me?" She frowned, then looked down at the nice outfit she still wore. "Well, it's worth a shot." As she wriggled through the window, she wondered what they might find inside. The police had already combed through the place, she doubted they left much behind to discover, but it didn't hurt to take a look. Once inside she unlocked the back door of the garage so that Mary could join her.

"What if Carlene shows up and finds us inside?" Mary began to look around the garage.

"We'll just tell her the back door was open, and we thought she was inside. Honestly, I'll be surprised if she even decides to show up. We have to find something to either link Brody or her to Graham's death, or Marlin's accident. If we can't, then she's going to take off and we might never find out what really happened to Graham."

After a few minutes of searching the nearly empty garage, Suzie paused and looked over at Mary.

"I think we're looking in the wrong place. Maybe we should look in the office. There might be some kind of evidence there. There's a door that leads to it over there." She began to walk towards it.

"Right behind you." Mary turned on the flashlight on her phone to give them both better lighting as they entered the office. It was just as cramped as she recalled, but most of the papers and storage boxes had been removed. The large, wooden desk remained, along with a filing cabinet, and a few shelves.

"It's been cleared out." Suzie frowned. "Let's take a good look around, hopefully we'll find something. Maybe under the shelves, or hidden behind a drawer." She began to look through the filing cabinet.

Mary ran her hands along the frame of the desk in search of any hidden compartments. When her fingertips bumped something smoother than the rippled wood, she froze.

"Look, there's something hidden back here." She did her best to edge the desk away from the wall. "I can't quite reach it." She shoved her hand in the space created as far as she could, but her fingertips only grazed the edge of the thin device taped to the back of the desk.

"Here, let's pull it out further." Suzie grabbed one side of the desk, then waited for Mary to grab the other. Slowly, they eased the desk away from the wall far enough for Mary to reach behind it and pull the device free.

"It looks like a small laptop." She frowned as she set it on the desk. "Whoever it belongs to definitely didn't want it found."

"Three guesses who it belongs to." Suzie raised an eyebrow as she opened the computer. "This is Carlene's desk."

"How could the police miss this?" Mary narrowed her eyes. "Wes is always so thorough, but I guess it was the crime scene techs that did the search, but they usually do a great job as well."

"They probably didn't move the desk away from the wall." Suzie tapped the keyboard. "It has a password." She sighed. "I doubt we'll be able to get into it."

"Wait, what was the name of that gang that she's supposed to be in? The one that Brody also belongs to." Mary eyed the computer screen. "Maybe she would use that."

"Let's give it a shot." Suzie tried a few different combinations of the name of the gang. On the fourth try, 'southcannon1' went through. "Got it! We're in."

"Fantastic." Mary glanced over her shoulder. "Did you hear something?"

"Hmm? No." Suzie began to navigate through the programs and files on the computer.

"It was probably nothing." Mary shrugged as she turned back to the computer. "What did you find?"

"There's some kind of program on here. I've never seen anything like it. It's a frequency reader? Frequency? Didn't Kline mention that the keys might have been cloned from reading the frequencies?" Suzie's eyes widened.

"He did." Mary nodded.

"Oh Mary, we've really found something here. If this program can copy the frequencies of the key fobs for the cars, I bet that's how all of the cars are being stolen —"

"Congratulations, you finally caught up." The voice drifted from the door of the office.

The hairs on the back of Suzie's neck stood up as she realized who it was. She turned to see Carlene in the doorway of the office.

"Mary." Suzie grabbed her hand. "I think we have a problem."

"Oh yes, you do. A big one." Carlene stepped the rest of the way into the office, then pushed the door shut behind her. It was a small space to begin with, and with the desk pushed out of place, it was even smaller. "I knew I should have waited a while longer before I brought the laptop back."

"Carlene, we were looking for you." Mary cleared her throat.

"No, you weren't. You were looking to cause me

trouble." Carlene looked between both of them. "Every step of the way you've been too involved in this situation."

"We'll just be on our way." Suzie grabbed Mary's hand and started towards the door that led back into the garage.

"No, you don't." Carlene casually pulled a gun from her waistband. "It was so cute when you were so scared of Marlin and his gun. He wouldn't harm anyone. I tried to convince him to actually, but he wouldn't go for it."

"You tried to kill him." Mary stared at her. "You cut the brake lines on his car."

"Sure, I did." Carlene shrugged. "He was a problem, and I had to solve it. You see, he figured out that I killed Graham, and he was going to turn me in. I tried to talk some sense into him, but he refused to listen. So, he had to go. It's a pity he didn't die though, now I have to finish him off as well." She pointed the gun first at Mary, then at Suzie. "Too bad you two won't get the same offer of a chat first, I know better now than to waste my time."

"Listen, Carlene whatever happened here, there's always a way out. You can make a deal with the police if you turn yourself in. Tell them what the gang made you do." Suzie tried to meet her eyes, to see if there was any trace of humanity left in her.

"What they made me do? You still don't get it. I'm the one that calls the shots, no one else. You see, I had a pretty good thing going. I copied the frequency of the key fobs for certain cars that the gang wanted, and then they were able to use that information to make a fake fob. They didn't even have to break in, just walk up, press the button and unlock the door. Pretty sweet, right?" Carlene shook her head. "Then Graham started to get suspicious. He thought it was Brody at first, then he became suspicious of me. He was always preaching to me about being a good person, and good things will come to you, blah blah. Nothing good ever came to him. He was alone when I met him, and he was alone when I killed him." She smiled a little as she looked between them. "But you two, you're not alone, are you? You have friends. Mary, that detective is your boyfriend, isn't he? And, Suzie your cousin wears a badge, too?" She pursed her lips. "There's not a chance I could let the two of you live. I can't believe you even showed up here tonight. Another stroke of good luck I suppose." She glanced at the clock on the wall. "We'll just wait until the next train rolls through, and then take care of things. As much noise as that thing makes, no one will even hear the gunshots."

"Carlene, this is a bad idea." Suzie took a step towards her. "We're not going to tell anyone."

"Keep quiet!" Carlene sighed, then rolled her eyes. "I really don't know why you had to ruin everything. Graham did the same thing. We could have both been rich, but he had to be so stuck on his morals that he wouldn't take the cash I offered him. Now, I've got quite a mess to clean up. It's such a pain." She pointed the gun straight at Suzie. "I'd love to kill you right now, don't tempt me."

"Suzie, watch out." Mary tugged her back, until they were both behind the large wooden desk. She grabbed one end of it, then looked over at Suzie, who nodded and grabbed the other end. After an unspoken countdown, both women used all of their strength to flip the large desk upward. As the wood collided with Carlene, she was too startled to shoot, and since the office was so small, it was impossible for her to get around it.

Suzie and Mary ran through the door that led into the garage, then headed for the door that led out to the parking lot.

"We won't have long, we have to get out of

here!" Mary gritted her teeth and ignored the pain that shot through her body as she ran for the car.

"Oh no, the tires!" Suzie gasped as she saw that the two front tires of the car had been slashed. "Mary, we have to find somewhere to hide." Suzie grabbed her hand.

"No, there's no time." Mary looked over her shoulder as Carlene jogged out of the garage with the gun in her hand. "The SUV!" Mary gasped and dug through her purse. "I have a spare key, hurry!" She tugged her towards the SUV. She had just managed to get in the driver's side and close the door when a shot rung out. Suzie dove into the passenger side, and pulled the door shut as Mary started the engine. It sputtered at first as if it might not start, then roared to life. The sound caused Mary so much relief that she actually smiled, despite Carlene firing off another shot. Mary threw the SUV into reverse and drove towards the back of the parking lot. As she switched to drive, Carlene continued to run after them. Mary's stomach churned as she realized she might have to run the woman over in order for them to get away.

"It's okay, Mary, we don't have any other choice." Suzie reached over and squeezed her hand. "We have to get out of here!"

"I can't." Mary shuddered at the thought and blared the horn. Maybe the loud noise would be enough to startle Carlene into giving up.

Carlene raised the gun, pointed at the windshield, and stared straight at Mary as she began to pull the trigger.

"Now, Mary!" Suzie shrieked as she leaned across the interior of the vehicle in an attempt to protect her friend.

A gunshot rang out, glass shattered, and shrieks filled the air. Suzie had her body curled around Mary's as she began to register that the shrieks were not screams but sirens.

"Mary, are you okay?" Suzie lifted her head enough to gaze at her.

"Yes, I think so." Mary looked up as well. "The windshield, it's not broken."

"No, the side mirror is." Suzie looked towards it, then past it, to Carlene on the ground. The gun was a few feet away from her, her leg had obviously been shot.

Wes ran towards Carlene, with Jason only a few steps behind.

Jason and Wes handcuffed Carlene, who writhed on the ground. They quickly handed

Carlene over to the uniforms and turned to Suzie and Mary.

"How did you know, Wes? How did you find us?" Mary asked.

"It wasn't me." Wes looked at her, his eyes wide with determination and a trace of fear. "I finally managed to track down Brody and I picked him up. He told me everything, that he had nothing to do with the murder, that it was all Carlene. Apparently, he worked it out after the murder. He said that Carlene got the bruise the night before the murder, she fell and hit her head. When he found out that she said she had been hit over the head, he knew that she had done it. That she had murdered Graham and pretended to be attacked herself. He was worried about turning her in. She's ruthless. Then we tried to reach you both, but there was no answer. I called Paul to see if you were with him, and he told me you were due to meet with Carlene at the garage to pick up the SUV." He stared at her for a long moment. "Mary, are you okay?"

"Yes, I'm okay." Mary took a deep breath. "Thanks to you, and Jason, and Paul, and Suzie." She realized how lucky she was to have so many people who cared about her. "Carlene killed

Graham, and she tried to kill Marlin, and she was going to kill both of us."

"Yes." Wes narrowed his eyes.

"That was terrifying, but we're okay, Mary." Suzie looked into Mary's eyes.

"Yes, we are." Mary straightened up as medics arrived to tend to Carlene.

Suzie could still see the barrel of the gun pointed through the windshield at Mary. As she turned to face her friend, she found Mary with her arms open, ready to hug her. Suzie wrapped her arms around her and squeezed.

"Remember how we were going to be more careful?"

"I remember." Mary laughed. "We've got to work on that."

"Yes, we do." Suzie smiled at her, relieved that they were both safe. Graham's murderer had been found, and justice would be served.

The End

ALSO BY CINDY BELL

SAGE GARDENS COZY MYSTERIES

Birthdays Can Be Deadly

Money Can Be Deadly

Trust Can Be Deadly

Ties Can Be Deadly

Rocks Can Be Deadly

Jewelry Can Be Deadly

Numbers Can Be Deadly

Memories Can Be Deadly

Paintings Can Be Deadly

Snow Can Be Deadly

Tea Can Be Deadly

CHOCOLATE CENTERED COZY MYSTERIES

The Sweet Smell of Murder

A Deadly Delicious Delivery

A Bitter Sweet Murder

A Treacherous Tasty Trail

Luscious Pastry at a Lethal Party

Trouble and Treats

Fudge Films and Felonies

Custom-Made Murder

Skydiving, Soufflés and Sabotage

Christmas Chocolates and Crimes

Hot Chocolate and Homicide

Chocolate Caramels and Conmen

Picnics, Pies and Lies

DONUT TRUCK COZY MYSTERIES

Deadly Deals and Donuts

Fatal Festive Donuts

Bunny Donuts and a Body

BEKKI THE BEAUTICIAN COZY MYSTERIES

Hairspray and Homicide

A Dyed Blonde and a Dead Body

Mascara and Murder

Pageant and Poison

Conditioner and a Corpse

Mistletoe, Makeup and Murder

Hairpin, Hair Dryer and Homicide

Blush, a Bride and a Body

Shampoo and a Stiff

Cosmetics, a Cruise and a Killer

Lipstick, a Long Iron and Lifeless

Camping, Concealer and Criminals

Treated and Dyed

A Wrinkle-Free Murder

A MACARON PATISSERIE COZY MYSTERY SERIES

Sifting for Suspects

Recipes and Revenge

Mansions, Macarons and Murder

NUTS ABOUT NUTS COZY MYSTERIES

A Tough Case to Crack

A Seed of Doubt

Roasted Penuts and Peril

HEAVENLY HIGHLAND INN COZY MYSTERIES

Murdering the Roses

Dead in the Daisies

WENDY THE WEDDING PLANNER COZY
MYSTERIES

ABOUT THE AUTHOR

Cindy Bell is a USA Today and Wall Street Journal Bestselling Author. She is the author of the cozy mystery series Wagging Tail, Donut Truck, Dune House, Sage Gardens, Chocolate Centered, Macaron Patisserie, Nuts about Nuts, Bekki the Beautician, Heavenly Highland Inn and Wendy the Wedding Planner.

Cindy has always loved reading, but it is only recently that she has discovered her passion for writing romantic cozy mysteries. She loves walking along the beach thinking of the next adventure her characters can embark on.

You can sign up for her newsletter so you are notified of her latest releases at http://www.cindybellbooks.com.

Made in the USA
Columbia, SC
18 June 2020

11370325R00117